A Stud's Love

A Stud's Love

A Lesbian Drama ...

A Novel

D. L. Collins

iUniverse, Inc.

New York Lincoln Shanghai

A Stud's Love
A Lesbian Drama …

iUniverse books may be ordered through booksellers or by contacting:

iUniverse
2021 Pine Lake Road, Suite 100
Lincoln, NE 68512
www.iuniverse.com
1-800-Authors (1-800-288-4677)

Because of the dynamic nature of the Internet, any Web addresses
or links contained in this book may have changed
since publication and may no longer be valid.

This is a work of fiction. All of the characters, names, incidents, organizations, and
dialogue in this novel are either the products of the author's imagination or are used
fictitiously.

ISBN: 978-0-595-45081-7 (pbk)
ISBN: 978-0-595-89392-8 (ebk)

Printed in the United States of America

This book is dedicated to My Mommy and My Brother
We did it.

Special Thanks

Taking a deep breathe I am so excited that it is finally over. I completed my first novel. I have so many people to thank but my first thanks goes to our Father and Savior Yashua the Messiah for without him breathing, walking, talking, and writing would all be impossible. I am so thankful that his works through me are as powerful as they are.

My babies Christian Dasean, Chris'Tion Jaylen, Trevaugn Joseph, Taylor Evaun, and Brooklen Jaye are my inspiration. I live for those 5 little people. My life without them would be incomplete. This is all of our dreams and Mommy makes sure that dreams come true by any means necessary. I would like to thank my sisters Charlisa and Angie … we have been through so much these past years but we are all strong and survival is not an option for us is it necessary … none other can compare to the bond that we have grown to have loving them is amazing I wouldn't trade any of our hardships for the world…. My niece and nephews Quanysa, Marquan and Torey … you are all the light of my life I look at you all grow and it amazes me to see you all grow up looking just like us when we were kids…. thank you for completing me and supporting me throughout my life struggles and now successes.

Thank you to the love of my life, everything I do is for us Baby keep being the star that you are in my sky. Markica Taylor you are the missing piece to my puzzle and I am proud to finally say my world is perfect because of you. I love you and our son Jaylen Trevon.

I want to give another special thanks to a special man in my life … I will never forget the talk we had and you told me that you feel like you were put in my life for a reason and that is to be my confidant. That you are and so much more. I appreciate you for the kind words and the faith that you have in me. You asked me not to forget about you when I'm rich and famous and my answer to that is how could I you are an important force in my life. Believe or not Tony Isa I respect you more than you know and I thank you for believing in me and lifting me up each and every time I have been down.

Last but not least thank you to My Dad (Charles). My Dad (Jamie), my sister Shauntice, my niece Ajanae, my aunt Deborah for giving me and my children serenity and peace of mind, I owe you so much and I love you for not leaving me out in the cold. This was a long hard road for me and I truly thank you for everything. Aunt Pam, Aunt Edna, Aunt Sandy. Uncle Jackie, all of my cousins, and friends who has been through the struggle with me I thank you. Thank you to my number one road dog Blaq(Autumn) we do it big round deez parts *smiling.* Thank you to all fo my Fridays (Southfield) Co-workers I love yall and I appreciate all of your support.

Introduction

Hello my name is Neko Jones, Fonzie for short I adopted my nickname in high school. Everybody said that I was the coolest mutha fucka walkin. I pretty much kept quiet over the years always had a flock of girls following me, people wondered why but, I never would tell. My cover up for bein in the life was to keep a man by my side, until one year I decided that it was time out for the secrets it was time for me to come out of the closet be who I really was. The only person that stood by my side was my best friend Lloyd. He stood by me through it all, even encouraged me to be me … that's because it helped him with pullin the ladies (just kiddin) but anyways, once I was out the closet I was out, I played women left and right until I met the woman of my dreams then it all came to a halt, well for a minute at least. Love is tricky and can hurt so many people with the slightest mistake. Life's a box of bullshit, at least mines was. Experience is the only teacher, and livin in the life taught me that real quick. Sometimes it takes a lot to learn. You don't realize life rewards until it's too late. Slowly I've learned to accept things the way they are and truly exist. With that I will tell u my story.

Wake Up!

This mornin' I took a real good look at myself and I realized that in my eyes … everything is not so bad after all. Sometimes you stand to fall…. somethings that are thrown may hit you in the face, black yo eye, make you cry, wanna die, ask that man why…. when in reality you know why. So act like you know and struggle to be strong, strive fa life long. Get a grip girl it ain't over. Life has just begun and that song you sung yesterday is none. I gotta open my eyes and see the sun past the rain it's killin me dang. I know that he loves me cause that's what I know and not only does it shows but the bible tells me so.

Stephanie

The sun was shining into my office window as I gazed down from the 23rd floor of the building watchin' the pedestrians enjoy the day. I wore a white Capri pants suit with a black tank complimented with black sandals that accented my freshly manicured feet thinkin' to myself what it would be like to have freedom. *Damn.... I wish I could say fuck this job and be enjoyin' the weather like everybody else ... but fuck it this pays the bills.*

In the middle of my thoughts I was abruptly interrupted ... "Excuse me Ms. Jones, I'm sorry I would have knocked but your door was cracked, I hope I didn't disturb you...." My receptionist said as she peeked into my office.

"Oh no your fine" I responded, "I was in my own world, I've had a lot on my mind lately that's all.... what's up?"

Her voice sounding concerned she informed me that the boss was waiting in his office to see me.

"Oh, well your boss wants to have a word with you as soon as you get a chance."

What now I was thinkin' to myself * he's always tryin' to get me in that damn office.*

"Ok thanks." I responded out loud.

My boss was an asshole, he was very persistent. He had been trying to get in my pants since the first day I stepped foot into the office. Just that past weekend he had given a Memorial Day celebration which I showed up with "my friend" and he seemed to be very upset behind it.

As I walked down the hall to his office, I began to think.... *what the hell do he want, I hope he not about to talk about my way of livin' I don't wanna have to get ignorant with this man. I come in do my job and that's it.... shit ... I even dress like they want me to. He betta not say shit about what I do off his time.* I approached the secretaries desk and everything about her face read trouble she said in a nervous tone, "Oh hi Ms. Jones, go on in Mr. Thompson is expecting you."

"Ok thank you Lydia ... how's the family?" I asked, I don't know why but that's a typical question in the business world, it's like a respect thing.

"Oh they're fine.... thanks for asking." With nothing further her eyes veered back to the computer where they were when I first walked up.

I walked into the office and the ambiance was the same, this time I had all of a sudden became sick with the bubble guts, my nerves were a wreck. I gained my composure before speaking, "Well hello Mr. Thompson, I heard you were looking for the infamous." I said jokingly. He didn't crack a smile.

"Uh yeah have a seat Ms. Jones this won't take long at all."

I sat knowing that something was wrong. * What the fuck * I thought to myself, I began to get nervous. "Ms. Jones the company is makin' some changes, we are downsizing and getting' rid of a lot of positions to keep from filing bankruptcy."

"Ok" I said looking kind of confused not knowing where this conversation was going.

"Well your position is one of the first to go." "Soooo ... what does this mean for me? Where will I be placed?"

Well that's just it we don't have placement for you, you're job has been fulfilled altogether. We have no place for you here ... I'm sorry."

I became furious, overwhelmed with pain, I knew it was because of my lifestyle and because I wouldn't give in to his sexual advances. "You're sorry" I said angrily "You're sorry ... your not sorry and none of you Uncle Tom muthafuckas are sorry. I'm not your typical workin' black showpiece.... I'm gay and you scared of that, be real wit me. Don't feed me wit no baby spoon be real ... you know what you can't be real.... why ... cause you'sa hoe ass nigga living for the white man.... but it's cool though.... I ain't mad I'll get over it...." I paused for a minute to try to gain my composure but it didn't work. "I should fuck you up but I'm not I can see the intimidation all in your face. I'm gone go pack my shit and bounce. You be good, enjoy life...." I walked towards the door I turned back and said "yeah and tell yo' wife I said I had a good time the other night and uh the breakfast was a great way of showin' her appreciation" I slammed the door.

Lydia was scared to lift her head as I gracefully walked towards her desk, "Lydia you take care of those babies and I will see you in the world aight." She looked up from her computer and said, "Oh of course Ms. Jones and I wish you the best." I smiled at her to assure her that I was fine "You know I'm good."

As security walked me thru the hall back to my old office to pack I thought * I can not believe this hoe ass shit, all I try to do is be what deez bitches want me to be and I still got fucked.... he probably just mad cause I get mo pussy den him * I laughed out loud and shook my head * Fuck it.... I guess ... it was time for me to bounce, stop tryin' to live fa deez muthafuckas ... Damn I called him a bitch.... I got real ghetto on dat ass *.

As soon as my truck hit the gates of my community I felt the weight lifted off of my shoulders. I couldn't tell you where my next move would be but I knew I would be tight. I had been well off for years do to hustling. Working for Compuware's cooperate office was a scapegoat for the crooked money I had inherited over the years.

My doorman greeted me as he always did when he saw my truck pull up. He was used to my routine, come in the house and remove my uniform (that's what I called my work attire) and head straight to my bedroom for a shower. Whatever he would have laid out for me would be what I would wear for the day. "What up dawg! What u doin home so early, I wasn't expectin' you til later on this afternoon?" He asked. "Yeah I know, dem bitches fired me." I responded soundin' pissed "But fuck it you know I'm good, dem hoes ain't did shit."
"Yeah, I know dat but dayum how long was u wit dem?"
"For a minute.... shit almost five years. But you know they ran some old getting' rid of yo position type shit when we all know what the real deal was."
"Oh word."
"Hell yeah."
"Dayum ... well look man I'll have yo stuff sat out when you come out the bathroom cause...." Before he could finish I interrupted "Oh you tight my dawg, I know I'm early just hook me up some lunch man I'm hungry. I'll get my own fit."
"Aight."

Lloyd was my doorman's name; we grew up together in the mean streets of Detroit, the Linwood area. We both decided to make a career out of the hustle but always have something' to fall back on. I was the brains of everything, I went to business school and he went to school to be a chef, he could cook his ass off. He would always tell me don't find a woman cause if I did he would be out of a job. I assured him that he would always have a job with me regardless to who came into my life. I thought about a relationship but all the women I had come across were crazy. Me and Lloyd would size females up. He's a good lookin' dude, light skinned, short brush waves, about 6 feet four inches, 196 pounds, and built like a model for Sean John underwear and me, light brown, shoulder length hair, 5 feet 6 inches, 168 pounds, and every femmes dreams. I would bring women over to see how they would react to pretty boy Lloyd (is what we called him). If they were to giddy then we knew that she was a fucker not a keeper.

I stepped out the shower and lotion my body with Izimiaki after shower lotion and sprayed my clothes with the cologne. I dressed in a navy blue tee with a red one to follow it, some Sean John jeans and some custom made navy blue and red Air Force Ones. I threw on a white du rag with a blue and red NY baseball cap. Lookin' good as usual I was determined to let go of all of the bullshit that was clutterin' my mind. Me and Lloyd sat in the kitchen and kicked it over lunch. "Man that bitch Keisha den called three times since you been indecent." Lloyd said shaking his head.

"Straight up what did she want?"

"She said she called yo job and they said you were no longer with the company, she questioning me and shit and you know what I told da bitch" we both said in together "Bitch suck my dick" we bust out in laughter. Those were Lloyd's famous words when he felt somebody was on some other shit. "Right, Man what the fuck I can't have no p-time, but she was suppose to braid my hair today, I ain't even gone let her do it."

"What about Janae?"

"Yeah, man.... but you know how I hate to be in between her legs. She be askin' for a commitment." We both started laughin'. "Females crazy." Lloyd said "Especially the ones you deal wit."

"Yeah man" I responded. "Well look I'm outta here man, I'ma go get my hair tight and hit a happy hour somewhere.... I'ma take the Monte so pull the Hummer in the back garage for me."

"Aight."

"Can I get another Dry Martini?" I asked the bartender as I sat in Mitches thinking on my next move. "Yeah well someone wants to buy this one for you." The lady bartender informed me smiling like a teenage kid. "Oh aight, tellem' good lookin'." "Alright."

I grabbed her attention before she walked away "Who is it doe?"

"She said don't say who she is she will talk to you when she get up the nerves."

"Oh well dats what's up."

"She thought you was a dude but I told her u wasn't, that's what made her skeptical you know she's my girl and she says she "strictly dickly." I started laughin' "Yeah that's what they all say, but you know how that go."

Yeah I know, but she'll be down here.... maybe." The bartender walked away sassy like.

It was only about 7pm so the bar wasn't crowded but it was full. Everybody was getting there after work drink. Beautiful women were everywhere so it was hard for me to point out the culprit. One thing for sure it was a lot of women there about their business. I sat at the bar and had two more drinks, as soon as I went to pay my tab a voice came over my shoulder. "I know you not about to leave and you don't know who I am." I turned around only to face the most beautiful woman in the bar.

"I know you didn't expect for me to wait … it's been two hours and two drinks later, I ain't the one to wait around I make shit happen." The woman laughed cocky but cute then replied. "Yeah I feel that."

"So whassup Ma, thanks for the drink I would love to repay you."

"Oh no need it was a friendly gesture. I thought you were nice looking and it looked like you had a lot on your mind."

"Yeah I lost my job today and I'm just trying to regroup."

"Sorry to hear that … what did you do if that's not being too nosey?"

"Oh naw you straight, I worked for Compuware's cooperate office. I was under the VP."

"Oh damn I know u sick."

"Yeah" I shook my head not looking for sympathy but just tryin to show her some type of emotion.

"By the way I'm Stephanie." She grinned as she held out her hand. I then extended my hand. "Aight Steph I'm Fonzie." She began to laugh again the same way she did the first time she approached me. "Fonzie huh that's cute but what were you born with?"

"Well the name I was born with is no longer my legal name, it's Neko, I got my name changed when I was 18."

"Why?"

"Because it wasn't me you know."

"Oh ok so what r u goin to do. I mean about yo job situation?" "I dunno, but I'm gone do sumthin', my bills don't stop, baby I gotta stay grindin' you know."

"Yes I do.... well if I could be of help I would be glad to grace you with my presence when you need someone." A big smile crawled across my face. "I would be glad for you to ... so look let me add yo' number to my phonebook and give you a call cause I got a run to make before it get too late."

"Alright, but umm you gotta woman or sumthin', I mean.... well ... cause I ... well ummm ... forget it"

"What ... u wonderin why u can't have my number?"
"Uh of course not"
"It's good Baby, I get that a lot, I really don't give out my number, I don't like to be bothered unless I wanna be that's all ... I den had to change my number too many times cause females don't know how to act. They be on dat stalkin shit."

"Oh ok, well that's not me"

"I know that's what they all say, then next thing you know I'm goin through some extra ass drama" I responded as she gave me a flirtatious laugh. "But look I really got something to do so I'll call you, but hay if something about me got you feelin fucked up in some kind of way don't do it. Baby I'm a real cat, prolly the realest cat you will ever meet, I don't play no games you feel me." I continued my statement.

"Yeah, I feel you, I mean but if you have a woman that's cool, I've never dated a female before so I don't know how this works. I found you very attractive and I just wanted to get to know you." She said with the most innocent face I had ever seen.

"Well look Ma, like I said if you feelin uncomfortable I understand it was nice meetin you, Naw I ain't got no woman but, I can't sit here and keep tryna convince you either, so what's good?" I said as I stood up out of my chair and grabbed for my Carhart.

"586." She started to recite her number.

"7721 oh 15"
"Aight den Ma I'm gone holla back atchu."
"Ok."
"You be good ma" I said as I started toward the exit.

"Alright"

No soon as I walked away from the bar I could hear the bartender start to interogate her. "Girl what happen" I could just imagine her with her elbows on the bar and her chin in the palm of her hands being all ears.

"I don't know, all I know is she is fine as hell, and I can forget that she is a girl real fast." They both started laughing.
"That bitch is a pimp I'm telling you she smooth as hell. You betta be careful girl she den had a plenty of 'em sprung. Shit why you think I stay away from her ass?"

"Girl shit I can believe it, and guess what they call her ass?"

"What?"

"Fonzie bitch."

"Hell naw." they both broke out laughin.

Soon as I hit home I was greeted with my house shoes. I went into the den to contemplate how I was going to approach this situation with Stephanie. This shit took skills. Dealin with females was sometimes a job in itself, a hard job at that but fuck it somebody had to do it. I called Lloyd into the room before he left for the night. It was Thursday and that's usually when his weekend begin. He stayed in the house with me but a lot of the females he dealt with wouldn't understand his job so he had an apartment downtown that he used Thursday thru Sunday as a get away. Plus when a female see you got money they tend to get dingy but If they know you got a lot of money they get psycho. It was very few women he brought to the house; he entertained people on our level at the house.

I paid Lloyd swell, more than the average doorman. We grew up together, when we were young he was the only cat that understood me and didn't try to change or judge me nobody could pry us apart we was like Siamese twins you wouldn't see one without the other.

Lloyd came into the den looking like he was goin to a jazz concert or something. "What up doe?" He said and sat on the chaise lounge that sat adjacent to the window.

"Damn Mr spiffy where you goin to see Kenny G or some shit dawg" I said laughin' being sarcastic making fun of his attire.

"Fuck you." He said as he adjusted the cross that hung from the platinum chain he had around his neck, what the fuck you call me for?"

"Awe shut up you sensitive ass nigga ... I called you in here cause I need yo advice on dis chick I just met."

"aight"

"Well she straight for now" I said bein serious but havin to laugh at my confidence.

"Listen to yo vein ass." Lloyd had to respond to my nonchalant attitude.

"Anyway so I told her I lost my job and shit you know told her where I used to work and all of that but I left out the fact that I had the business and all that. I don't want her to look at me for what I got you feel me." I explained to Lloyd.

"Oh of course that's whats up."

"But she seem cool, so I wanna see where her head at, so do you think I should ..." Lloyd quickly interrupted.

"Man get a room tell dat bitch you moved all yo shit in storage until you find something a little more in yo price range and play dat bitch like dat, if she feelin u den she'll be bout it." He finished his sentence as if it was a done deal.

"Dayum dawg it's like you be reading my mind I couldn't have said it better myself. The thing is I don't wanna stay in no bullshit feel me?"

"Well nigga you know how we do shit get a 6 month lease in my complex fuck it.?

"O hell yea hell yea, that's whats up. Hook me up dawg, you still fuckin the leasin agent?"

"Come on dawg you know I am shit I gotta keep the perks, don't wanna pay rent fa real." He said catchin my hand for some daps as we both broke out laughin. "I'll call her tonight you'll be in dat bitch tomorrow."

"That's whats up."

Friday morning I was up just in time for the moving company to come and pack my clothes and a few odds and ends to into my new place to make it look authentic. I decided to go to cort rental to order some furniture for the duration of my lease. "Just pack the clothes in the walk-in closet down the basement." I informed one of the workers.

"Ok sir, is that all you're taking?" She asked looking around the house hoping I would say yes.

"Yeah, and it's Ma'am but you can call me Fonzie." I corrected her with a phony smile on my face.

"Oh I am terribly sorry Ma'am." Her white face turned beet red from embarrassment.
"That's aight, it happens to me all the time I'm used to it." I reassured her.

They continued to get my things together as the men began to load up what was already packed and ready to go.

Back at the apartment Lloyd was taking care of my paperwork and waiting for Cort Rental to bring the furniture, my place had to look lived in for a while so his lady friend found me a unit where a couple had just vacated. No fresh paint or new carpet but it was kept up by the previous tenants all Lloyd had to do was bleach it down for me.

By the time I made it to the apartment after changing my address at the bank and on my identification card Lloyd had my place looking like me. That's one thing I have to say about him, he knew me almost better than me. I had to admit the place was nice but much smaller than I was used to. It was two bedrooms two and a half bathrooms with a small study. Ok for the average bachelor but I wasn't average. My house in Canton, MI was five bedrooms, one den, four bathrooms, finished basement which could pass for a whole other house, with an indoor and outdoor pool/Jacuzzi. I looked around the apartment, the living room and dining room was connected. It was furnished with an olive green couch and chair, a red chaise lounge with Mahogany wood end and cocktail tables. My dining room set was a mahogany wood with high back leather chairs. It fit me totally and completely and it made me look like the average Joe well I mean Joann.

I picked up my cell phone and dialed the number Stephanie gave me as I stood in one spot and looked around the house familiarizing myself. I knew that it would be a chance she would just be getting off of work because it was a little after five. "Hello." The voice answered on the other end spoke.

"What's hatnin, is this Stephanie?" I asked already knowing that it was, how could I forget the sound of her voice.

"Yes it is, who is this?" She responded in a sophisticated tone.

"Dis Fonzie."

"Oh, wow." She said sounding surprised. "I mean hello … I mean um what up?" We both couldn't do nothing but laugh.

"Nothin much, what I surprised you." I knew I did but I wanted to hear it from her.

"No, it's not that it's just that I didn't expect for you to call me for a while." She said sounding as if she was used to men playin those same childhood games.

"Why not, I'm not a teenager anymore, I'm grown as hell I don't have to do the 2 week test, I told you if I like it I go for it before it's gone." I could tell that she was blushing on the other end of the phone cause it took her a minute to respond.
"Yeah I hear you talking Ms. Fonzie." She finally responded.

"Oh ok so you are a little black huh?" I said being sarcastic as usual.

"What was that suppose to mean?" She said soundin as if I offended her.

"Well I mean you be talking all proper and shit I thought you was a good girl or one of those high saddity chics."

"I mean I am a good girl but, I can be bad too."
We both started laughin.

"That's what I'm talkin about ... so whats up when can I see that person you know take her out or something?"

"I don't know but, I'll take you out tonight." She said confirming that she was game to see me just as much as I wanted to see her. I paused for a minute not knowing how to respond to her wanting to take me out.

"Oh aight so um where do you wanna take me Ma." I said in a joking way.

"Wherever it doesn't really matter to me, it's the weekend lets just do something."

"Aight so what you want me to come get you?"

"Naw can I come to your house cuz it's complicated to get to my house ... everybody seems to get lost coming all the way out here to the boondocks."

"And where might the boondocks be?" I asked curious to know what she considered the "boondocks."

"Monroe."

Even though I only stayed about 30 minutes from Monroe I played it off like she was right. "Oh hell yeah, you stay far as hell, you can just come to my house, I stay downtown in the River Bend Town homes."

"Oh ok I know exactly where that is, so how about I see you at around 9:30?"

"Yeah that sounds cool."

"Alright I'll call you when I am at your building."

"Aight bet." We ended our conversation and I spent the next couple of hours familiarizing myself with the light switches, the water settings and all the little shit the apartment had so that it would seem as if I had been staying there for awhile.

Right when I stepped out of the shower my phone rang. I looked at the caller I.D. and seen it was Kiesha, I started not to answer it but, I had avoided her long enough, besides if I wouldn't have answered she would fuck up my whole night. "What up doe?"

"Neko where the hell you been?" She instantly caught an attitude when I answered the phone.

"Girl what the fuck I tell you about callin me dat?" I said getting just as mad as she was.

"Look nigga I was yo first, I have that right."

"Yeah, ok don't get fucked up.?

"Anyway, why you have me waiting for you yesterday and didn't come get yo hair braided, I coulda been doin other shit besides waitin fo' yo' sorry ass, and you could have told me you left Compuware."

"Girl I'm sure yo ass still did whatever it is you was gone do and second of all I ain't gotta tell you shit we are no longer together girl get that through yo thick ass head."

"Yeah well nigga who braided yo shit? Mya?"

"Damn there you go, none of yo business." Right then before she could comment my line clicked "Girl hold the fuck on." I demanded.

"Yeah aight."
I clicked over on the other line. "What up Doe?"

"Fonzie?"

"Yo."

"I'm in your complex Sweetie, this is Stephanie."

"Aight, my address is 15901 River Bend Dr.… just keep straight to the first stop sign and make a left I'm the second set of townhouses."

"Ok I'll see you when I park."

"Aight Baby cause I ain't dressed yet I got caught up on this damn phone."

"Oh ok that's no problem."

"Aight." I clicked back on the other line not even wantin to hear Keisha's voice. "Well look Babygirl I gotta go."

"Neko, I miss you, when can I have some time?"

"I'll call you tomorrow." I responded after she sounded so sweet, disappointed she smacked her lips before she responded.

"Alright den." We hung up the phone and as soon as I threw on my boxers and wife beater Stephanie was at my doorbell. I buzzed her in, as soon as I seen her I knew she would be wifey. She was wearing an Azzure halter top that was

made like a sweater with some Azzure jeans that fit every curve perfectly. I immediately had second thoughts about going out I wanted to sit up under her and
enjoy her company. "So what up Ma, what you wanna do? Where you wanna
go?" I said actin silly tryin to break the ice.

"I mean it really don't look like you tryna go anywhere with no clothes on
Miss I'll see you at 9:30." She responded sarcastically but in a joking way.

"Naw Babygirl I jus …" she cut me off.

"It's ok … if you want we can stay here, I mean have you ate?" that's when I
knew she was ready for the killa.
"Naw, but we can watch some movies and order something from Pizza Popa-
lis." I suggested.

"We can order movies but I would rather cook for you, I love to cook what
you got?" Stephanie said sealing the deal on the whole wifey thing I mentioned
earlier.

"Oh straight up, you gone cook fa me, Awe shit you tryna be my woman."

"Is that right?" She laughed.

"Fa sho.?"

"Well you know that's just me, I aim to please baby." She said with the biggest
prettiest smile I had ever seen.

That night we ate broiled Salmon, redskin potatoes and asparagus, we popped
a bottle of Dom P and drank a pint of Absolut Cranberry. We were sitting there
watching White Chicks when I started to lay my head across Stephanie's lap.
"Why do I feel like this, why do I like you? She questioned sounding confused, I
sat up out of her lap and looked her in her face. "What? What do you mean, I m
not likeable?" I said putting my hand on my chest like I was appalled.

"No I'm not saying that." She said with a smile. "All I could do was think
about you and then when you called me I was extra excited I wanted to see you
right then, I've never felt like this before … especially about a … well … um a …

I'm sorry I still get choked up even saying it, no offense." She said noticeably being embarrassed.

"No you aight, that's cute doe, I like you too." The sexual tension filled the air. Her nipples were bulging threw her shirt and my boxers were moist. I leaned over to kiss her lips as she submissively obliged. I started to unbutton her pants and pull them slowly below her waist. "I've never done this before." She moaned as I kissed in between her thighs. "Just relax." I responded assuring her that I had total control of the situation. I clamped my hands tighter around her hips sp that she wouldn't squirm all over the place as well as to make her feel secure that I was goin to take care of her. I slowly moved my tongue over the bareness of her pussy. I went from using my tongue to strategically kissin her until I reached the lips of her wetness and in a circular motion I started to caress her clit sucking passionately. As she let out low moans her body started to shake. Her moans became louder as she moved her hips to the motion of my tongue, her head lifted up off of the couch and her back arched ever so perfect as I clinched a hold of her waist tighter and sucked harder while she began to explode all in my mouth and over my face tryin to fit her mouth to tell me to stop but the feelin was so good she couldn't get it out. "I am so sorry." She whispered almost being ashamed as she tried to scoot away. "Don't be sorry Bay its aight." I reassured her. "Let me make you cum again." I got up and went to my bedroom as she lay curiously on the couch. I came back with my strap and her eyes almost popped out of her head. "I can't do this." she whispered nervously as if we were sneaking. "Yes you can Baby." I said "Turn around." I turned her soft body over and began to thrust my strap in and out of her wetness as she began to move her body to the beat.

"OH my god Neko, you feel so good, please don't stop."
Our lust lasted until the early morning.

CHAPTER 1

▼

SABRINA

A year has passed since I had first met Stephanie, we had made it almost official the night of our grand opening for Studz, a barbershop/topless bar that me and Lloyd decided to open. The plan to open the bar had been in the making for about 5 years we just had to find the right location; this is all we used to talk about growing up. We found a spot in Downtown Detroit in The Lofts. It was the nicest spot ever, it was equipped with two floors, sound proof doors, 14karat gold railing going up the spiral stairs with Navy blue marble floors ... yes I said Navy Blue. Everything was custom made, that's just how we was, the originators, that's what we used to call ourselves as kids and it stuck wit us through our adulthood. It was something we said amongst ourselves.

The grand opening was so off the hook that we had decided to open another one just like it in Atlanta but we had to go scope out the areas and find the right spot. Stephanie was so happy; she had been supportive in every way. Financially, she had put up 20 grand, of course that was before she knew anything about me having money. I had so much more in store for her though, I longed for her to be Wifey.

Throughout the night I had DJ play specific songs and a messenger drop special gifts at her table. The first song of the night was Slow Down by Valentino, I had a dozen long stemmed red roses sat at her table with a note that said I love you. That was the first time I had ever said it, I mean she had told me all the time but I would always say "I know". She would call me an arrogant fucka who's lucky to have her in my life and in my heart I always knew she was right. I watched from a distance and she was so elegant, the smile that came across her face was the most beautifullest thing in my world. The second song that played was "All My Life" by K.C and Jo Jo, I had a bottle of Dom sent to the table with a note beside it that said "If I could look back and change anything about us, it would be nothing". After reading the note she gracefully blushed and nonchalantly looked around to try and spot my location, I knew at that moment she felt like a princess, that made me feel good, she had been there with me thinking I had nothing, she deserved it all. The grand Finale would top everything off, I had a big box delivered to the table before the last song was played with a note that read "There are 10 boxes here, one inside another, one gift representing each month we've been together. The biggest one remind me of your huge heart and the smallest box is a thank you, thank you for lovin me." As she began to open the last box the DJ introduced the group Jagged Edge and they performed their hit single "Wifey" as I kneeled on one knee and of course she said yes.

The excitement for us filled the room, that's when we became official. I took her to our home in Canton and she was amazed, I told her from this day forward you will never have to work again. She was overwhelmed, she held her face and cried "This is all too much Nek, where … what have you been doin behind my back?"

"Bay this was all me before you." I explained "I just got tired of people wantin me for this."

"Awe Baby, I love you, however you are, you are my world, I wouldn't know what I would do without you … this makes us so much more complete." She held her hand out as she stared at the four carat ring that fit perfectly on her ring finger.

The words she spoke touched me in a way I had only dreamed of before I wrapped my arms around her waist and kissed her soft lips. She melted, as much as I wanted to lay her down I knew that her night had been long and she was tired, I ran her a bath and waited in our bedroom until she got out and fell asleep with our bodies intertwined.

I walked in the house to the smell of bacon frying. Stephanie had taken complete control over the kitchen. Me and Lloyd would only be allowed in if we were.... Well never. She told Lloyd his job was now limited, of course he didn't care, his salary stayed the same and we were makin a killin at the shop.... in a minute he would be leavin us anyway. I walked behind Stephanie as she cooked and grabbed her by her waist; I had been out early takin care of business. "Hay Baby ... you hungry?" She asked as she enjoyed the kisses that I placed on her neck.

"You know I am baby, always ... where's Lloyd?"

"He said he had to go run some last minute errands before yall leave this afternoon."

"Oh, ok."

Me and Lloyd were headed to Atlanta to push up on a deal we had made with owner of "Decisions" an alternative club. I had met the owner when I worked for Compuware, he was feeling me so I played my hand. He thought Lloyd was my man so we had to leave it that way besides I didn't want him tryin to get at me. Stephanie had never seen me dress feminine and I wanted to keep it that way, so when she packed my bags she packed me as usual and as usual Lloyd would go out and shop for me for our trip. I would never show Stephanie that side of me. It was irrelevant I only did it for America anyway.

"Baby I'm gonna miss you while you're gone so hurry up and come back." Stephaine said as we were loading up the cab to go to the airport.

"Oh that's the only person you gone miss bighead?" Lloyd responded sarcastically. We all laughed.

"Awe nigga shut up you know im'a miss yo big head butt." Stephanie and Lloyd had become close almost like sister and brother.

"Aight Bay you be good while I'm gone, I don't want no shit." I said putting the last of the luggage in the back.

"Come on now you know better than that." Stephanie responded, I kissed her as passionately as I knew how. "I love You baby girl."

"I love you baby girl." Lloyd mocked.

"I love yall too." Stephanie laughed.

The plane landed at the airport and I approached the exit. "Thank you for flyin Delta sir." The attendant said flirtatiously.

"You're welcome." Lloyd responded bein funny, we both knew she was talkin to me.

"Oh I'm sorry I meant your friend, but you to sir."

"Well in that case you meant Ma'am." I interrupted; the woman's face was blush red with embarrassment.

"Oh I am so so sorry, I mean as long as I've been in the life I should have known." She commented makin sure she let me know that she was in the life, probably bi-sexual I was guessing.

"You good Babygirl … I get it all the time…. So um whats your name Ma?"

"Oh it's Sabrina."

"Aight Sabrina, I'm Miss Jones, I'll be stayin at the Marriott maybe I can see you a little later."

"Oh Ok."

"Aight then the room is under Lloyd Stevens." I ended the conversation, Me and Lloyd walked away bawlin. I had left the attendant with something to think about.

Me and Lloyd always had conjoined rooms so that we could have our privacy when necessary. "So do you want me to send ol' girl over here when she come?" Lloyd asked.

"What makes you think she is goin to come?" I questioned wit a smirk on my face. We looked at each other at the same time and said. "She gone come."

"Well yea if she come on yo side send her my way so I can put the mack down on her." I started laughin.

"Yea aight nigga." Lloyd mumbled before he left the room.

I jumped in the shower to get a quick rinse and thru on some skin tight jeans and a metallic tank top that hung low in the front to show my cleavage. I loved myself; I was sexy however I chose to dress.

I began to unravel my braids so that it could look naturally curly. Looked in the mirror and in less than an hour I was completely transformed, ready for our meeting which started in less than 45 minutes. I walked through the double doors over to Lloyd's room.-

"What up nigga you ready?" I asked as I strutted into his room showin off my girlish figure.
"Dayum mu fucka you looking straight bitch, if I ain't know you I'd have you." Lloyd said bein funny. Lloyd was sexy as hell too, he always dressed nice and smelled good, if I didn't love woman so much I would mos def put it on him.
"Yea it seems like every time I dress like dis, my pussy contract when I'm around you." I responded with laughter, keeping the joke alive.
"You silly man, you ain't ready fa dis!" Me and Lloyd joked all the time about hookin up but we knew that it would never go down, we were like family.

We arrived at "Decisions" just five minutes before the meeting. Mr. Tolbert was sittin at the bar flirtin wit one of his bartenders. As I approached the back of his chair, I placed my hands over his eyes. "Guess who?" I said in the most seductively disguised voice. The bartender instantly caught an attitude and began to roll her eyes until she seen Lloyd, then she became distracted.
"Well let me guess … it's gotta be my favorite lady Miss. Jones." Mr. Tolbert responded. I lifted my hands off of his eyes.
"Yes Baby you know it's me in the flesh … whats goin on witchu?"

"Nothin much Miss Jones you looking good and gracefully aging ... how old are you now 21?" we both laughed.

"Yea so that makes you 30 huh?"

Mr. Tolbert was in is early 50's and me well, lets just say I got about a couple of decades to be where he is. "Well Miss, so what's to talk about, have you come up here with a plan Ma'am?"

"You mean "we" Mr. Tolbert ... you remember my fiancé don't you ... Lloyd?"

"Oh yea how are you youngin?" He asked. He knew exactly how to get on Lloyds bad side. Lloyd disliked Mr. Tolbert cuz he tried to play Lloyd like a chump. Even though Lloyd was not my man if he was he would have been a real sucka for the stuff he had seen Mr. Tolbert do.

"I'm aight olden." Lloyd responded with a grimace. "Now lets get down to bitness besides ain't that what we here fo?"

"Yea we are ... so what have you two decided now I mean cuz I'm ready to get this paperwork done so I can move to Florida with the wife. She's been buggin the shit outta me since I said I was sellin the place.... Now you know I'm askin 45 thousand that's including the liquor license right?"

"Now come on Mr. Tolbert we agreed on 40g's when I talked to you last, what happened?"
"Well look here, what you got and we'll see?"

"I told you what we have so let's get this shit over wit ... me and Lloyd are tryin to plan a family, I am ready to go home ... we came down here to get this over wit."

"I don't know Ms. Jones, I've had offers on this place that is mighty fine ... I was tryin to work a deal wit you." Lloyd seen the anger in my face, I had never been good at keeping my boyish ways on the inside. I was ready to go off. Lloyd immediately took control of the conversation.

"Man look do what you do cause we got 35g's and we'll gladly take it some-where else ... you talkin that shit about you Fam nigga my girl told you off rip what we had, so are you telling me we waisted a trip.... Man fuck dis nigga ... come on Bay let's go." Lloyd began to walk towards the front of the bar ...

"See Tolbert you got my man mad at me and you ... Ima go home to some ..." before I could finish Lloyd interrupted.

"Come on Baby I ain't got time for his shit ... we'll go somewhere else period."
Lloyd played his role so good I almost believed him, shit for a minute I thought I was gone go home and get my ass beat.

"Alright, alright Babygirl to save yo family just give me what you got and let's get this paper started." Mr. Tolbert said getting frustrated.

"See Bay he's gonna take the 35."
He came back over towards us and we began to deal.

No soon as we walked into the hotel lobby from the meetin the front desk clerk called out. "Mr. Stevens excuse me sir."

"What up"

"There is a lady in the Captains bar waitin for you or she said a Ms. Uh ... Jones ... I'm assuming that's you?" She looked over towards me. "She said that she would be there for awhile."
"Ok thanks." Lloyd responded before we started walkin towards the bar.

"Well man Ima go and get dressed for dinner and uh what you want me to do come and get yo ass from the bar?"
"Yea my nigga let me see what ol' girl talkin about."

"Aight den."

I walked into the bar and spotted Sabrina instantly. It was funny she reminded so many ways of Stephanie (her physical appearance I mean) I walked toward her thinking *I'm always meeting a broad at the bar, damn, she better be talkin bout something.* "Hello Miss Sabrina." I spun her chair around as she start blushing.

"Hi Baby, you look good, better then you did earlier … I get a chance to see what your working wit."

"Oh yea." I said laughing.

"So you never told me your name Miss Jones."

"Oh, I didn't did I, it's Neko …"
"That's cute."

I instantly got stuck, when she said that it took me back to the day when I first met Stephanie, when I told her my name was Fonzie she said the same thing. I thought to myself *Damn that was some freaky shit.* "Yea thanks." I said out-loud.

We talked about everything from music to movies to travel, we had so much in common. "You know I'm originally from Detroit." Sabrina told me.

"Oh yea, what part?"

"The Westside … I still have family there, I moved here to get away from the scrutiny from my family because of my lifestyle … my parents hated the fact that I left my husband for a woman, they couldn't understand me and the feelin's I had for that girl, I mean I haven't givin up on men I just don't feel them like I do woman. You know to my parents my sister was "Miss. Goodie two shoes," she was happy wit her man and she was a proper bitch so you know how that go … Mommy and Daddy's baby."

"Yea I feel you."
"Yup me and my sister don't even talk, I think that's a damn shame … we're twins and you wouldn't even know it by our differences our parents ripped us apart … I feel sad a lot of days." Sabrina sighed and began to look sad before she started to speak again. "I hear that she's doin good though, she's engaged and all that but that's all I know. I heard from a mutual friend so she really didn't go into detail. I didn't really want to hear it, I really just…. Well I mean I miss our bond but I'm straight you know … she decided to treat me dif'rent cause of our people and that's crazy to me."

"Yea, well what does she think overall of your preference?" I asked bein concerned.

"She has always agreed with my parents on everything, Stephanie doesn't have a mind of her own, she wants to make everybody happy but her. I don't understand her. We used to be so close until my parents found out about me. We even used to have talks so I know how she feel about women, she's just scared to admit it to everyone."

"Who ... Stephanie ... that's your sister's name?" I asked now being a little more curious, the biggest knot was in my throat, I tried to swallow but it was almost impossible. I started to think to myself *This cannot be happenin, this is not Stephs twin ... naw whats the odds of that happenin ... calm down Neko you're just paranoid*

"Yea dats my sister's name, I mean like I said I hear she got it goin on now but I haven't talked to her in years."

As soon as I went to respond Lloyd walked into the bar. "You ready my dawg?" He stopped and noticed Sabrina. "Oh, my bad nice to see you again Ma."

"The same here." Sabrina responded.

"Yea I'm ready." I said as I turned to Sabrina to let her know that I wanted to see her again before I left.

"Where are you guys headed so soon?" She asked as if she didn't want me to leave.

"We have a couple of more things to handle before we head out ... we just bought a club here and so we have a lot of last minute things to clear up."

"Oh, ok ... well take down my number and of course I know where to reach you at while you're here ... it's 717-552-5253."

"Alright ... can I get a hug?" We hugged and she kissed me on the cheek.

"I'll see you soon." She said as she started to walk toward the exit.

"Alright Sweetie."

I couldn't wait to get in the cab to tell Lloyd what has just happened to see if he felt the same way I did. "Man guess what the fuck just happened to me!" I said sounding anxious.

"What?"

"Sabrina, I can't fuck wit her."

"Why not, man she look good as hell she almost remind me of Stephanie."

"Nigga, that's the problem." I said getting even more excited.

"What nigga? Awe hell naw don't start trippin' like you all in love like that cause you den proposed and shit." He responded like he was disappointed.

"Naw nigga it ain't dat."
"Well what den?"

"I think dey twins."
Lloyd looked surprised, one of the first times he had ever been speechless. "Shut the fuck up Dawg ... how you know?"

"Man look I ain't even lyin ... we was kickin it and she told me about her family and why she left and blah zay spleat ... and she got a twin name Stephanie that sound just like mine.... And why I kinda think it is her cause every time I talk about my fam she don't never mention hers.... so I gotta find out. Nigga dat shit would be crazy if they were doe." I said laughin nervously while curiosity raced thru my head.

"Word ... nigga dayum that's some freaky shit dawg."

"I know right?"

"Yea so what you gone do? How you gone find out?"

"Man Ionno I gotta figure sumthin out doe."

"Hell yea."

As I packed my clothes getting ready for my flight back to Detroit the phone in the room rang. "Ms. Jones" I answered in my most sophisticated voice, I knew that it was business cause Stephanie only called my cell.

"Well do you think you gone have time to see me before you leave Lady?" the voice asked on the other end of the phone. I was shocked that she called me; I must have made a helluva impression.

"Um sure, my flight don't leave for another 6 hours ... I was just packin though ... you can come now if you want to cause I have a run to make before I go to the airport."

"What a coincidence I am down the street, give me about 10 minutes aight."

"Ok."

Sabrina reminded me of me except she was feminine but she was gangsta, she talked with a twist. I liked that. She didn't hold her tongue. I could see myself takin a liken to her just cause her style was untouchable.

She arrived to my room and knocked at the door, I opened it and there she stood, looking good as hell, the man in me wanted to come out but I had a plan so I had to be as feminine as she. She wore a Lakers jersey dress that had slits everywhere but there, I wanted to attack her on sight. "I'm glad you could make it." I said.

"Im glad I made it." She responded with the same flirtatious smile she gave me when we first met. I went to close the door behind her and when I turned around she began to kiss me. She caught me off guard, so much was goin through my head at once, I was used to be the aggressive one. Thought started rushin thru my head *awe shit I hope she don't think it's goin down*but as she stepped back and removed her dress and revealed her navy blue lace bra and g string my thoughts instantly changed. I shook my head and thought to myself *yup it's goin down* I had never had a female give me head before and I knew that's what she wanted. She started to kiss me again and I obliged. I took off my shirt and walked her towards the bed.

"Are you sure you ready for me" she whispered. I wanted to put my pimp hand down and ask her if she was ready for me so bad but to my surprise the bitch came out of me and said.

"Yes, all of you." She laid me back on the bed and started kissin and suckin in all the right places. I was amazed at how good she made me feel I wanted her to keep goin, my mind began roamin again * is this how I be makin bitches feel?* As she lightly bit my inner thighs, my wetness was throbbin, I reversed the role and began to kiss her lips as she lay on her back. I messaged her legs and feet then began to gently suck her toes, she moaned.

"Oh Nikola, you feel so good" I moved up her leg with my mouth and placed my hand on her wetness "shhhiittttt" she moaned again. It turned me on, I had to taste it, I began to suck on her clit as she lifted her legs over her head, I ran my tongue down pass her split and into her backside, she begged for me to let her taste me and then exploded everywhere. She waited no time before she asked me to lay back, hesitantly I began to lay there.

"Whats wrong", she asked me as she tried to get me to relax.

"Nothing", I responded.
"Just thinking."

This was my first time ever havin this done to me so I was stuck but, I didn't want her to know that. She started to suck me like a pro and, in less than five minutes my body went into convulsions. We layed there in deep thought wonderin what next, holdin each other like we were totally in love.

Back at home Stephanie waited patiently for me to walk through the door. All the way home I wondered how I was gon find out if Sabina was really Stephanie's twin. Stephanie had never mentioned a sister before let alone a twin. My mind was once again racing. It seemed I didn't know Stephanie after all and maybe that s why she had cut her parents off. She wouldn't be able to face them now that she is dating a woman. Well, at least that's what she told me, you know that she had cut her parents off. I didn't know what was what anymore but, she would only have a minute to bring me up to speed or she would be another one of Fonzie's lost in love.

I walked in the house exhausted from the long day, after landing in Detroit I had to go get my hair braided by Tamika and you know what she wanted. Of course me bein me, I couldn't turn her down, besides I missed her and she was a dime. She wasn't totally ready for me though, she wanted her cake and eat it too, so I had to cut her loose and only hit it every once and awhile.

Stephanie greeted me with the warmest hug, "Haay Baby I missed you so much".

"Whats up Ma, I missed you too".

"Where's Lloyd Baby"?

"He's takin the stuff out of the trunk. I am so tired Bay, can you get me ready for bed"?

"Bay you already know that is takin care of, your joint is on the soap dish and your drink is bein chilled. I just turned your water off like 5 minutes before you walked in, so it still may be too hot, you need to tell Lloyd to go turn that water heater down that water gets way too hot Bay".

"Aight, well bring me my drink in about 10 minutes Baby and I'll talk to you when I'm clean".

"I love you Baby".

"I love you too Sweetness". I responded outloud but in my head I was really thinking *do you* I mean she was the perfect girl, she made sure erthang in my life ran smoothly. It took her some time to adjust to my ways but when she did it was all good.

I soaked in the bath thinking about how I was goin to approach Stephanie with the informationI had learned about. I hit my joint and closed my eyes, I couldn't quit get with the blunt thing that was for the young kids two or three puffs with my drink and I was straight … well not straight but you know what I mean. * what the hell am I gone do, I wanna get to know Brina but what if Steph … man fuck that I can't be thinking like this* before I could finish my thought Stephanie walked in with my drink.

"Baaaaby, here you go".

"Thank you sweetheart, I want you to stay in here wit me".

"You ready for me to wash you up already"?

"Nope not yet, I just want to see you".

"How was your trip"?

"Is that what you call a trip? It was business".

"I mean well you know".

"I'm sorry, didn't mean to snap I just have a lot on my mind".

"What happen, you got the building right"?

"Yea but that's not it, it's us.... Ionno yo people and it just be botherin me, what the fuck how we gone be together for this long and I really don't know nothing about you"?

"Baby that's not true … what do you want to know, I told you my parents are old fashioned or I don't want them to treat you dif'rent, they know about us if that's your worry".

"Man it's more then that".

"Well what bay?"

"I mean I don't know if you have any brothers or sisters, nieces or nephews. Do you want kids, I mean what?"

"I don't know if I have any nieces or nephews, I have a sister and no brothers, I mean I didn't think it was that important, I mean since me and my sister haven't spoke in years, since we were about nineteen. Nine years ago she left the state, I really don't know why. I mean I love her with all my heart, were twins, her and my parents didn't agree on things and I don't know, I mean … this is a tough subject for me, I try to act like she don't exist so I don't hurt as much but, believe me it's hard." Stephanie began to cry, I felt bad that I even brought the subject up.

"Don't cry baby, it's ok. I said and kissed her gently on her lips … come here." I grabbed her by the arm and pulled her towards the tub. All she wore was a baby

T and some panties when she would wash me up. Her nipples standing at attention she began to remove her panties and then her shirt. She say in between my legs as I began to rub her shoulders. She laid her head back on my shoulders and moaned my name. "Neko." I ran my hand down her breasts and pinched her nipples until her hips started to grind in motion. "Baby." She said "I love you." I placed one hand in the water on her wetness as the other one pinched her nipple. Gently my hand ran across her clit, as she grinded my hand her eyes began to close and she began to explode. I began to squeeze the water from the washcloth down her breast as she lay there motionless. My job was complete, I got the confirmation I needed without leading on that I knew something.

CHAPTER 2

▼

NO MORE SURPRISES

Strange feelins had began to come over me, I had been seeing Stephanie and Sabrina for months now without neither one of them catching on. Most of my time was spent in Detroit but, my weekends would almost always be In Atlanta. I now had a home in both cities. Actually, two in Detroit, the home me and Stephanie had together and I had leased another apartment through Lloyd's girl for when Sabrina would come and stay in Detroit with me. She had a key and everything so she thought that she was my one and only, and I wanted to keep it that way.

Lloyd had bought a house in Atlanta too so that he could run the shop there during the week. We would alternate so that things would run in both cities smoothly. Sabrina had became a major part of my life, I couldn't see myself livin without her it was weird but, I loved her. We had started to talk long term. "Baby I really think you should consider movin down here wit me for good, I hate when you're away … I wanna wake up wit you every morning." Sabrina told me over dinner.

"Ok, so if I do that then what am I goin to do about the shop in Detroit."

"Well, I think you should hire somebody to run it or you and Lloyd work it out to where he goes o the "D" (that's what we called Detroit) and you stay here permanently … I mean cause we have so much here already." Sabrina was right, even though we had only been together for 8 months we had bought a house together, owned 4 cars and was in the process of opening a Soul Food restaurant but, my life was still with Stephanie. That was my heart, I could truly be myself with her, I mean I could be myself with Sabrina too but it was just dif'rent. I wasn't really a Femme and I couldn't show Sabrina that, even though I wanted to. I wanted to be able to be honest with the both of them but, I wasn't willin to sacrifice losing either one of them. "Brina baby things will work out for us soon … just not now … me and Lloyd are doin things this way for a reason." I tried to explain to her. I knew that she was upset cause she jumped up from the table and went straight to the entertainment system and blasted the music, Fantasia's song "Free Yourself" came blastin from the speakers like we was at a club, she walked back over to me and pointed her fingers in my face and started to sing with the Cd. "If you don't want me then don't talk to me." She slightly pressed it against my forehead. "Go ahead and free yourself."

I began to get furious … so instead of getting mad, I got up and walked toward the door. Sabrina stood in front of me trying to prevent me from walking out and before she could say anything my anger was so deep I raised my hand and back slapped her with all my might. "BITCH DON'T EVER SAY FREE MY MUTHAFUCKIN SELF." I screamed. I couldn't believe I had let myself get that angry over a song. I guess I just wanted a reason to get away for awhile. I had been in Atlanta for almost 3 weeks, I had told Stephanie that things where in shambles there and I had to get them straight. Sabrina held her face in disbelief, I stormed passed her and hit the off button on the radio and as my back was turned I heard her screamin behind me. "WHAT THE FUCK IS WRONG WIT YOU." As she attacked me from behind. I finally got away from the tight grip she had around my neck and I slammed her to the floor. She laid there holding her face cryin. I went to our room and grabbed my car keys and some personals to walk out the door. "Where are you goin." Sabrina continued to lie on the floor cryin. "Don't leave me baby I'm sorry."

I didn't even look back, I knew I was wrong but I had to get away. I thought to myself * what the fuck are you thinking nigga, I know yuou ain't losin yo mind* as soon as I got on the outside of the door my phone rung, I thought it was Brina "What?" I answered with a attitude.

"Damn nigga it's like that, who made you mad?" The voice on the other end of the phone said.

"Who dis?"

"This Simone but if I caught you at a bad time I understand." Simone was a girl at had met at the shop in the "D". She was feelin me the moment she hit the spot before she even knew I was the owner. She tried to get a job as a dancer but we were fully staffed. I convinced her to go get her Barber License so she could cut hair in the shop. All of the Barbers were women, their attire were Barber capes and six inch heels. "Oh what up Ma, naw you good, what it do?" I asked.

"Good cause I need to see you."

"I'm in Atlanta right now can u wait until I get der'."

"What time is that?"

"I'm headed to the airport right now hopefully I can catch the next flight, if so at about 3 in da morning but if dat's too late then I holla at you in the afternoon sometime." I knew she wasn't gone turn me down.

"Naw 3 is good cause I really want to see you."

"Aight den I holla when I touchdown."

"Alright, seeya."

"Aight ... one."

I landed in Detroit at about 2 15 in the morning, I turned my phone back on and had 23 unheard messages all of them except for 2 were from Sabrina beggin me to come home. The other two was from Lloyd beggin me to call Sabrina cause she was interrupting him and what he was tryna do wit one of his hoes. I didn't feel like bein bothered wit Sabrina, I got straight in the cab to my apartment so that I could have Simone meet me there. As soon as I got in the cab I called Stephanie. "Hello." She answered the phone half asleep.

"Hay baby I miss you." I said feelin some since of relief to here her voice. I really did miss her and was anxious to lay in her arms but I had to see what Simone needed first.

"Baby?" She sounded wide awoke after she heard my voice. "I miss you too ... you r phone was off and your stupid voicemail was full so I couldn't leave my baby a message ... I have something to tell you Sweetie."

"I'll be home in the next day or two can it wait?"

"Of course baby anything for you." There was a slight pause over the phone, I didn't get quiet purposely I just lost my train of thought after she said she wanted to tell me something, I wondered what it could be. "Fonzie." Stephanie broke the silence.

"yo!"

"I love you." She told me, my heart began to smile, it felt good to know that she had my back and loved me unconditionally.

"I love you too Mommy ... You keeping it hot for me?"

"Haaaaayyyy." She responded, that was our little thing we'd do, I would ask her that after I'd been gone for a period of time and she would always respond like Fonzie on Happy Days. It always made me smile, that's why I loved her the way I did.

"Aight Baby ... I'll talk to you tomorrow."

"Alright."

I hung up the phone from Stephanie and called Simone, our conversation was short and sweet. I told her to meet me at my apartment in the next 30 minutes, that would give me enough time to change back to Neko. I powered my phone back off so that I wouldn't have any interruptions and no sooner than I got situated Simone was at my door. I opened with my boxers and T-shirt on. "Whassup Ma." I asked her as I walked to the kitchen to get me a Corona. You want a beer?"

"Nope. What else you got?"

"Um, what you want? You know I got what you need." We started laughing.

"Gimme some Remy den nigga."

"Aight, you want it wit Dom?"

"And you know this man." Simone giggled after she commented; she knew that I would always criticize her slang. I stood in the kitchen to fix her drink while she got comfortable on the couch. "So how was your flight?" She asked.

"Long as hell, a lot on my mind." I said as I walked out the kitchen with our drinks in hand. "It might be strong but you know how we do?" I handed her drink.

She sipped it once and said. "Oh it's fine."

"So what up doe, what you want to talk about that couldn't wait until the morning?"

"Oh my goodness Fonz what happened to your face?"

"What?"

"It's a big ass scratch."

"Oh shit me and Lloyd playin around and shit."

"I was about to say ... where dat bitch at?" We started laughin.

"Oh naw it ain't shit like dat."

"Alright now." She said as she playfully rolled her eyes. "Well anyway, you know that I have been tryna get my license to cut hair so that I can work in the shop right."

"Yeah."

"But its not working fast enough Fonz ... I got three kids and this shit is really a struggle."

"How is that Simone, I pay fa all that shit and yo child care so whats up, you only got a little ways to go."

"I know Fonz but, it's hard I don't get no help from their dad, I need a job I can't keep bein out here like this man, let me just work upstairs in the bar part time."

"Man hell naw I told you I didn't want you up there wit dem girls man you better than dat. You got potential baby girl."

"You think so." She started to get teary eyed.

"Man I know so … come here." I reached out and gave her a hug. "Now look my day was long, I'm tired as hell but I'ma tell you tonight what I'm gone do … you gone finish school, girl you only got a few more months to go. Im gone drop 10 more gs in your account and that should hold you for a minute, so all you gotta do is focus on getting back and forth to school and if that don't work let me know."

"Alright. And you still gone pay my childcare?"

"Fa sho, I got you."

Simone hugged me tight and started cryin tears. "Thank you sooo much Fonz … I love you." I grew to like Simone and her style. She was a good girl who had been hurt by several dif'rent men, all I wanted to do was see her make it with her kids.

"So do you want to stay here tonight? I'll sleep on the couch." I asked her, I had never tried to come on to Simone, I respected her and knew that mentally she was goin through a lot.

"You don't have to give up your bed for me I want to sleep with you, I don't bite you know. I know you got a Wifey or a girl but you have done so much for me, I owe you, I wanna lay wit you, can I?" Her eyes were so sincere.

"Baby you don't owe me shit and even if you did I wouldn't ask you to do that."

"But I want to." She stood in my face so close we may as well have been kissin.

"Look …" before I could get the words out we were kissin, unable to control the passion I grabbed her neck from behind and kissed her with every bit of anger I had in me. I sucked her neck with such force it was bound to leave a territorial mark. She moaned softly in my ear just enough for the warmth of her breath to arouse me even more. We laid on the floor as I removed her clothes. I reached up under the couch for my strap and without puttin it on I sucked on her wetness and slid it in and out of her as her juices began to squirt everywhere. Simone begged me to fuck her harder. "Don't stop Daddy please you feel so good." Her body began to run away from me as she shook uncontrollably. I forcefully grabbed her back towards me with one hand as the other hand continued to push the strap inside of her harder. I started to suck on her clit again until her moans became pleasurable chants. "Oh my ... what the ... wait a minute I'm about to cum!" Her hips began to grind faster as she had reached the highest point of pleasure, allowing her juices to cover my lips and chin we lay there.

"WHAT THE FUCK IS GOIN ON?" I was awakened by a slap in the head. "Girl what the fuck is wrong wit you." I said angry that I had been awakened so early. Sabrina had caught a flight to Detroit and walked in on me and Simone lay across the floor sleep in the nude. Simone woke up abruptly standing up fully nude tryin to cover herself wit her hands. "Oh my god is this ..." Simone pointed at Sabrina coverin her mouth. "I am so sorry." Simone had seen Stephanie a few times down at the shop so she assumed that's who Sabrina was. I looked at Simone with a look for her to just be quiet. "What the fuck is goin on Nikola!?" Sabrina was full of anger, Simone looked confused as I responded.

"Look chill out aight go in the room until I come in there and let me talk to Simone."

"Sa who? Fuck dis bitch who is she?"

"Look girl do what the fuck I said." I was tryin my best not to call her by her name, Simone interrupted. "Um look, I am sorry. I don't know whats goin on ..." She looked at me with a weird look as she questioned the name that Sabrina had called me. "Nikola".... let me out and you do what you do." I wanted to take Simone outside and explain but I had to calm Sabrina down.

"Simone jus go ahead and go and I'll talk to you later aight?"

"Hell no you want talk to her later, this bitch is a has been how da fuck you gone play me." Sabrina added her two cents. I grabbed her by the arm and forced her into the room while Simone left out the door.

"What the fuck are you doin here girl?"

"No the question is what the fuck are you doin here? Is this what you do? Huh muthafucka ... come home and fuck Simone. That whore bitch? Oh my god and the bitch ain't even cute." Sabrina was furious, at this point I knew she was jealous, Simone was cute as hell. She was about 5'4 143lbs she was light caramel with flawless skin. She was the shit, Sabrina knew it and it scared her.

"Come on Brina, Simone is a friend of mine. I looked at her like a sister until last night." I tried to calm her down but it only made her even madder.

"A fuckin sister ... yeah Ok you DON'T fuck your sister Nikola." Sabrina said cutting me off.

"If you would let me finish ... Dayum."

"Go head this shit is interesting ... huh ... yo fuckin sister?" She chuckled "You are fuckin hilarious. What the fuck next with you Nik? Sometimes I sware you should have been a nigga."

"Look she had a problem and so did I ... we fucked aight, it happened ... so what can we do? You mad?"

"Nikola" Sabrina said in a whining voice as she began to cry. "I want you to come home wit me. Fuck Detroit, come home baby ... wit me." She started to cry louder, I felt so bad. I was in love wit Brina ... well Nikola was anyway but it was so complicated cause I loved Stephanie too. I wasn't ready to let my life with Stephanie go not for something that wasn't even all the way real. I had gotten myself caught up in a game that I started and seemed to be losing at it in a fast pace. I could not disappoint Sabrina so I told her I would do just that. "Well look Bay let me get things situated here first ... things are in shambles and Lloyd is busy working in Atlanta. He can't just stop what he's doin to come here. So look as soon as erthang erthang den we gone do dis. Ima get somebody fulltime at the shop and I'm comin home for good." I couldn't believe I was letting that lie come out of my mouth.

"You mean it Baby?"

"Yeah I can't stand to see you like this girl, you know you my heart."

"I'm trustin you Baby." We started to hug as if nothing had ever happened.

I had dug myself in a deeper hole. The shit ws getting complicated, and I knew that some way or another I had to find a way to get out of this mess I had created. I had to get out of this "big move" but then again maybe not. Could I really pull off livin a double life?

I stood in front of my house and with a deep sigh I said to myself * aaaahhhh ... home sweet home* I knew that as soon as I walked into the door I would be greeted by the warmest most loving hug. It seemed like decades that I had been away when in actuality it had only been two weeks. I seen Stephanie's car parked in the entry way so that was a sign that she had just gotten in. "Honey I'm home." I put on my best I love lucy impression. Stephanie came runnin through the living room like the biggest kid. I loved and missed her energy so much. What we had was real. No one could ever replace her, not even if they tried. Just seein her joy started my mind to goin * am I really willin to give up all of this for a life in Atlanta ... with ... * I paused and started reminiscing *naw*

"Baaaaby I miss you." Stephanie said as she jumped in my arms and kissed me all over my face. "Baby I have the best news ... I can't wait to tell you." She was so excited I almost didn't want to interrupt.

"It's that good huh?" I questioned.

"Yes baby ... it is."

"Aight well um let me sit down den."

"Yea Bay it's two things.... Ok so first right ..." She paused. "How was your trip?"

"It was good ... now tell me your exciting news"

"Ok Baby you ready for this?"

"Yea Baby go 'head." I could tell she was anxious to let everything out at once.

"Ok first I talked to my parents. You know the talk we had that day has just been on my brain.... I know I know that was sooooo long ago but still it was on my mind strong and I had to call them."

"Aaaannnddd." I said anxious to hear the rest knowing deep down where this could lead to.

"And Bay ... they talked to my sister and come to find out she's been here in Detroit a couple of times and they say she want to see me just as bad as I want to see her ... my Mom ad Dad are learning to be Ok with whatever she chooses to do in life." My heart began to work overtime and my brain went racing * what the fuck* I thought to myself but my mouth said. "Well dats whassup Bay."

"Yea I know, I mean Bay like ... well I'm not going to ask you to meet her or anything like that yet because we have to get reacquainted, but I was thinking the next time she come I can bring her to the house and maybe ... well ... I don't know."

"What do you want? You askin me to leave ... I mean dats cool; I know you gotta spend time with your folk." I felt so much better, that was a close call, my heart began to go back to the normal pace.

"Will you do that for me Bay? That's why I love you, you are so sweet to me."

"Anything fo my baby.

"Thank you baby." Stephanie said as she hugged my neck. "Ok so guess what else Bay!" She said kind of bouncing up and down with more excitement.

"What?"

"Ok so right, you know how we had did that hook up a few months ago and I kept coming on my cycle.... so we said that we would just wait until next year or whatever?"

"Uh huh."

"Well um tell Lloyd to get ready to be an Uncle"

"What" I said with more excitement than she had.

"Yes Bay we are pregnant" she said as she started dancing. "We gone have a baby"

"Hell naw" I picked Stephanie up and hugged her as tight as my muscles would allow, then quickly sat her feet back on the floor afraid I would harm the fetus that was growing inside of her. "So Bay you ready for dis' ... I mean dis' is what we wanted right?"

"Yes Sweetie it is" Stephanie said as she kissed my cheek.

All of a sudden my mind went back to the reality of the situation, I was in a dilemma. My wife was pregnant, and my girl, who was her twin sister, wanted me to move to Atlanta permanently. To top it all off the two were getting closer to bein close again and, I was stuck in the middle. I couldn't stand for another surprise.

CHAPTER 3

▼

THERES THAT WORD COMMITTMENT

This is something me and Stephanie had planned ... I mean the baby and all but, it all happened so suddenly. Lloyd couldn't believe it when I finally reached him. "Man you did it" I told him as soon as he picked up the phone.

"Did what nigga?"

"Man she pregnant"

"Who now Man, deez hoes be telling you shit like dats gone change some shit and make me come back to the D man fuck dat, I'm straight" Lloyd instantly caught an attitude. I bust out in laughter before I responded.

"Naw man, I mean Stephanie Dawg"

"Get out"

"Yup nigga"

"Oh shit nigga I had a attitude at first" he said with a giggle. "Well that's what's up den nigga ... congrats Dawg ... so yall know how far along she is and shit?"

"Naw man she just told me when I came back home and shit ... but, the fucked up part about it is Brina want me to leave erthing here and move to Atlanta and I can't man, especially not now but, I can't tell her dat."

"Right ... shit man I don't know what to tell you ... nigga uh shit" he paused "good luck" he busted out in laughter.

"Yeah right … and guess what else?"

"What up"

"Brina in da D, we got into the other night and so I caught a midnight flight out … Dawg the next morning she walked in on me Simone clownin both our ass."

"Word"

"Nigga, hell yeah … look she tell Simone bitch bye" we both started laughin, I continued. "Nigga, Simone was so nervous … den look after I get ol' girl out the house Brina gone say and the bitch ain't even cute"

"Oh she was just hatin' cause Simone cute as hell"

"Right! But look den she gone say you need to move home for good she like fuck da D and erthang in it" We bust out laughin again.

"Yeah man she crazy, she was sick when she seen dat pretty ass young girl laid up wit her woman"

"Right but Dawg, dat ain't it."

"Dayum it's some more to this sexapade?" Lloyd questioned bein funny.

"Her and Stephanie plan on meeting sooner than later so now whats up wit dat? Brina den called her people and told dem she be in da D all the time now and she want to regain a relationship wit her family"

"Word…. It almost sound like you about o be powered down … Game over dude."

"Man fuck dat, it ain't over til it's over"

"Yea man I hear dat"

"Yeah well look Im'a hit you back, so look you make sure you prepare fa the worst and hope fa the best cause I mos def need some prayer on my side"

"Fa Sho my Dawg"

"One"

"One"

Once I hung up the phone wit Lloyd I began pondering on what my next step would be. I thought to myself. *Man what the fuck have I gotten myself into…. My world cannot crumble like this … something gone have to happen … shit*

I hadn't been to the shop in a while, so I went up there to see how things were goin. They never knew when me or Lloyd would pop in but, it was always on jam and shit was always goin smooth. Besides I had one of the coldest Studs in Detroit runnin my shit proper like. Her name was Blaq, she made sure no nigga or bitch ever got out of line in my spot. She was an ex cop so you know how that goes. She ended up leavin the force to work for me full time cause I doubled her salary … the force couldn't touch that. She jumped on my offer like it was Janet or Beyonce you feel me. "What it do Fam?" I said as I walked into the door. "Hay Studdaddy" one of the barbers commented "you looking real good in dem jeans and that tee baby"

"That's what I do … where's yall Popa?" I asked.

The barber smacked her lips before she responded "Now you know she back dare on nem monitors seein who just made the doorbell ring … stop it." We both started laughin.

"Oh dats what she do?"

The barber continued to laugh this time a lil harder "Naw nigga that's what yall do!"

I walked to the back of the shop where there was a steel door "The Castle" is what we called it. That's where erthang went down. From the money movin to the private affairs. You know like the old sayin "what goes on in the room … stays in the room." We even put bitches on punishment in the room, as a matter of fact I walked in on a punished worker at that very moment "What up doe cuzz" I asked as I looked around the room to make sure erthang was erthang, I mean I trust my dawg to an extent but come on now ain't that much trust in the world. Sometimes people get greedy. I wasn't worried though me and Blaq go way back. "What up doe my nigga" he responded as we showed each other some love.

"Why she standin in here looking like she just got her ass whooped or something?"

"Shit not yet, Ionno what I'm gone do wit her, shit nigga three days straight dis broad den said she ain't had her tip out cause she ain't been makin dat much choe right … den I catch da broad today all in a nigga face letting dis nigga feel er up and shit right … so I walk up to'em and say so dis nigga feelin you up huh, that must be for the three days of tip outs plus today right. So the bitch gone look at me stupid and say huh (she said in a girly voice), I told da broad I say get yo ass up and go to "The Castle" right … den I ask the nigga so what was it worth to you, he gone say man Ionno I got no money…." I interrupted.

"Hell naw"

"Right, so I tell da nigga to empty his pockets, so he looking at me like Im stupid, like Im a bitch right so I say it again do you know dis nigga had the nerve to say fuck me and he called me a bitch. Nigga I whipped my shit out so quick and said dis fa what nigga"

We both started laughin and slappin hands, Blaq looked over at the girl as if to dare her to even have a smirk on her face then we continued to laugh as she continued to tell the story "then I said now nigga come up out yo shit bitch and kick rocks ... Nigga I was so fuckin heated, first dis broad gone try to be a hoe on my dime den dis hoe ass nigga gone think I'm a bitch cause I'm a girl. Man he just didn't know."

"Man hell naw, dat shit was wild as hell, shit dat nigga lucky I wasn't here we'd a fucked his whole world up ... How long he been gone?"

"Shit about three hours, I just been havin her standin here and think about what she did" we both started laughin.

"Oh she on punishment ... you know like the kind yo momma used to do?"

"Exactly"

"Yea well we don't need nobody like dat here dats gone take from the family so let her walk"

"Well dare it is den it's a DD(done deal is the long term)."

After Blaq finished takin care of the former employee's paperwork we kicked it for about an hour or so, she caugh tme up on the finances and so on and so forth.

Back at home Stephanie received a phone call. "This is Stephanie"

"Hay Steph how are you?"

"I'm good and who is this?" Stephanie questioned not recognizing the voice on the other end of the phone.

"This Is Brina ... Stephanie"

"Brina" Stephanie was excited and overwhelmed at the same time "my baby sister?"

"That's right girl ... yo twin baby sister" Brina responded with the same tone of excitement.

"Hay whats goin on stranger, how has life been treatin you?"

"Everything is fine with me, how about you Ms. I'm engaged to the man of my dreams"

Stephanie started smiling really big with just the thought of marrying Neko "Yes and expecting our first Baby"

"Wow, are you that's great"

"I know, I can't wait I am sooo happy Brina. So when are you comin back to Detroit I would love to see you, we have so much to catch up on. I talked to my Baby about letting you stay at our place while he's out on business."

"Oh sis that's not necessary, I'm here in Detroit now but a friend of mines has her own place here and I am stayin wit her you know we are kinda like an item."

"Well that's good, how long are you planning to be here?"

"Um I really don't have a clue, maybe like a week or two. Just until she gets things situated with her business"

"Oh well that's cool, so are you driving maybe we can meet for lunch or something?"

"Yeah I am ... where do you wanna meet at?"

"Let me call Fonzie first, let him know whats goin on and I call you and let you know."

"That's cool I need to do the same thing so just call me with the details ok."

"Alright ... I love you sis and I'm so glad you called."

"I love you too." They hung up the phone both feelin the same relief inside. There parents had turn them against each other so many years ago all because of a sexuality that they both shared. One was just bolder than the other to come out of the closet.

As I was drivin down 275 South towards my house the automated voice machine on my phone rang Wifey into my earpiece alerting me that I was receiving a call from Stephanie before it atomatically answered the call. "what's good Ma"

"Baby guess what" Stephanie sounded ecstatic, more so then she did earlier when I had talked to her, I already had a feelin it was some more news about her family.

"What's up"

"My sister is here in town and ..." right at that moment I heard nothing else she was sayin my mind started to think all kind of shit fast *oh shit, she gone wanna take us out.... What if she say she wanna meet me.... Dammit what if she wanna stay wit us and try to talk Steph outta telling me to leave ... shit ... what the fuck am I gone do* Stephanie interrupted my thoughts when I heard her voice raise a little bit to get my attention. "Honey did you hear me."

"Huh, what ... I'm so sorry Bay what did you say I was tryin to listen to you and the radio at the same time" I thought of a quick excuse to get out of the fact that I was lost in my thoughts.

"Well listen to me Bay it's important."

"Ok Bay go ahead"

"Ok so anyway … she's here for two weeks and I told her that you was leaving and so me and her could spend some time together and.…" She was interrupted by my other line, the activated voice in my ear said My Boo. "Hol up Bay let me get dis" she smacked her lips and blew her breathe with impatience.

"Ok Baby hurry up."

I clicked over on the other line before it hung up "Whats goin on Ma"

"Baby what are you doin."

"Nothin, what are you doin"

"I'm at home waitin for you"

"Ok well, I will be there in about two hours, I have to make one more stop before I come to the house."

"Ok well hurry"

"Ok, Bye" I click back on to the other end of the phone "Ok Bay I'm back go head and finish."

"Anyway before I was rudely interrupted by whoever that was on your other line … it was probably Lloyd … I swear what would he do without you?" we both started to laugh "So how does that sound Sweetie"

"It sound good I'm happy that you guys are goin to spend some time together … I have to leave tonight anyway so I'm about fifteen minutes away from da crib, when I get there you can give me all the kisses and hugs Ima need when I'm away from you and then tell me all the stuff you got planned wit your sister aight, cause I know that's all you wanna do anyway." Stephanie chuckled before she responded.

"K' Baby … I love you and thank you."

"Fa what"

"For being mine."

"Awwweee you so sweet, I should be telling you that. I'll see you in a minute and I love you too Sweet thang." I hung up the phone and was smiling from ear to earthlike to myself *If you feelin like a pimp nigga gone brush yo shoulder's off*

When I got in the house Stephanie had my dinner on the table and my suitcases at the door.

"What's for dinner Bay?"

"I made your favorite next to your favorite … fried chicken, rice and corn."

"That's what I'm talkin bout, take care of yo Baby." I said pattin her on the backside.

"Bay I hope that you can start staying home more often now that I'm pregnant, I want to share this with you."

"Yea I know that's why I need to get shit right now cause I plan on marryin you before he get here and shit."

"Oh he huh? How you know it's a boy?"

"Cause that's all my nigga can make." we both started laughin.

"Is that right."

"Dats right Ma" I said as I hugged her around her waist and gave her a kiss on the cheek. I was starting to feel overwhelmed about the pregnancy, I felt like it was rushin the whole marriage thing, I mean it was a point in my life that I knew I wanted Stephanie to be my wife but now my life was getting complicated so now I wasn't quite ready for marriage. I was back and forth between two women that just so happen to be twin sisters. One I loved and the other one I lusted for and neither one of them was I tryin to lose. Things so far had been working in my favor, I could have Stephanie thinking I'm out of town while I spend time with Sabrina at the apartment. I would just have to pretend to Sabrina that I was so buried into my work that I had no time to really spend outside of the house. That way she would get tired of bein here and be ready to go back to Atlanta. I had shit all planned out. To me I was livin every mans dream except I was a woman.

I kissed Stephanie and wished her well with her sister before I left the house on my way to the apartment. I had to stop over to Blaq's house to change my clothes and take my hair down. Although Sabrina liked my braids too it took me outta character, sometimes I would forget much quicker which role I was playin.

Brina had company when I walked in the house, one of her high school friends that she had kept in touch with. Every time we touched down in the D Tyanna would be the first person at the crib. "Hello Tyanna" I spoke bein sarcastic I didn't care for her much.

"How are you Nikola?"

"I'm Fantabulous honey" I said shunning on the insides, sometimes I couldn't believe the words I let come out of my mouth. I was truly bein a girl.

"Well I'm glad to here that … so have you heard the good news about Brina and her sister?" Sabrina instantly caught an attitude.

"Dayum bitch can I tell my woman the good news first shit … you talk to damn much!"

"Oops … oh well sorry hoe."

"Yeah we know that … anyways Baby."

"What's up with you and yo sister?" I questioned as if I didn't know already.

"Well we are goin to see each other while I am here, I told her I wouldn't be here long though."

"Well that's cool can I meet her?" at that moment I was reversin psychology hopin that it wouldn't back fire.

"Of course Baby …"

My heart instantly stopped until she continued to talk. "But not just yet I want to spend time with just us first we have a lot to catch up on you know I mean I want to know what she's been up to. She already told me she's engaged and they're expecting their first child, I am really happy for her. She sounds in love."

I took a deep breathe to myself before I could speak out loud "That is so good, you know I totally understand, she does sound happy but I'm jealous though shoot I can't wait until we can get pregnant."

"Yeah well we need to get us together first." Tyanna said added her two cents into the conversation. "Now do you think you whores can get it together enough to do dat, I mean shit yall both sick in da head, and can't neither one of yall seem to stay faithful." We all started laughin except for mines wasn't sincere, that's why I couldn't stand Ty she always had something to say about everything and didn't care about what you thought.

"Shut up Ty fa we put yo ass out" Brina said and I agreed.

"Right" we all started laughin again.

"Sike you know I'm jus playin." Ty responded.

Me and Brina looked at each other then back at her and responded at the same time "no you ain't" the room filled with laughter again. Me and Brina went on jokin and laughin as if nothing had ever happened.

That night we all decided to go out and have a few drinks. Whenever we would go out we would always go over the bridge to Canada, I knew way too many people in Detroit and so what were the odds of me runnin into someone I knew in Canada. Shit somebody would definitely spot me in Detroit and then Stephanie would have my ass for breakfast lunch and dinner. So of course since we were all drinkin and Tyanna was the person she was (always analyzing shit) the subject came up. "Why we can't neva stay in the D shit yall love this Canadian shit, I don't be feelin dis shit over here … I don't be feelin like we fit in" Ty said wit her face all tore up.

"You know what girl I don't even know Me and Nikola have been comin over here since we've been together…. We never party in the D and I never asked why I guess cause I never thought about it but shit that's a good ass question … so why don't we Nik?"

O k now at this time I was on front, I was drunk as hell and had to come up with something quick but my quick wit thought fast even though I was intoxicated "Come on now Brina don't act like you don't know, you know I'm cheap as hell and always tryna save a buck … shit they say it's cheaper to keeper right" we all started to laugh.

"Oh you a trip … yeah but you right doe it is cheap as hell to drink over here." Brina commented.

"yeah it is" Ty agreed.

"And we still be havin fun feel me." I cleaned it up, we all shook our head and laughed in agreement. I was the comeback kid. I thought to myself * dis bitch gone try to front on me and try to get me all caught up … bitch don't front on me. She must ain't never paid attention to this pimp vein in my arm.*

CHAPTER 4

▼

THREES A CROWD

Three months had passed and Stephanie was finally in her third trimester of the pregnancy. She was 24 weeks and everything about her was beautiful. Sabrina and I were still holdin on strong to our relationship as she grew closer to her sister. We were still stayin in Detroit but I had been back at home with Stephanie. My days were becoming strenuous goin back and forth between the two of them everyday, the good thing about it was that they were so busy spending time with each other I was almost invisible.

I had finally talked Sabrina into goin back to Atlanta without me, she seen for herself that the shop needed me in Detroit. "The only way I'll leave is if you promise me you'll move home for good as soon as things are in order here." Sabrina said to me in the cutest baby voice.

"Now you know I will, I just don't want to leave and things get worst." I had made up this big story about the dancers in the shop and how we were looking for new girls to replace the old ones cause things wasn't goin right. Brina had drained me from my Detroit line. I was tired of changing face every single day, it was getting old and boring fast. Plus I just wanted to be normal and spend quality time with Stephanie. I needed that right now.

"Ok I will look into the next flight out this evening. I want to make a few stops before I leave."

"Alright well you know that I prolly won't be able to see you before you leave cause I have that meetin in a couple of hours so ..." she cut me off before I could finish my sentence.

"So what ... let's get it on." She said in her best Marvin Gaye voice. I chuckled as I walked up to her to give her a hug, that was my que to take her in the room and get but booty naked. We ended up doin for hours that if I did actually have a meetin I would have surely been late.

Stephanie had been complainin since I had been home about her stomach hurtin. I had gotten so frustrated that I had locked myself in the office I had built off of the back patio looking onto the pool area. I couldn't believe she was being such a baby, I mean but what should I expect she was carryin a whole other human inside of her. I was just frustrated overall. I couldn't begin to know how that felt. Even though I was a woman I couldn't imagine givin birth. I mos def would always leave that up to Stephanie.

"Fonzie, open the door." Stephanie hollered from the other side of the door "somebody want to meet you."

"Who is it Baby I'm busy?" I lied.

"Baby please ... come on."

"That's Ok if he's busy let him go ahead I will meet him sooner or later ..." When I heard the voice I was stuck, it was Sabrina. "Anyway I just came to say bye, I have a plane to catch."

"What do you mean ... you're leavin so soon?"

"Girl I've been here for almost three months it's time for me to go ... I don't have it like you miss thang I have to go home and make sure everything is in tact, shit I might not have no lights, gas, shit I might not have a house." they both started laughin.

"Girl stop it, you know you lying."

"Ok well I'm exaggerating but, I do need to get home though." They stood next to the door talkin like I wasn't even there I was thinking to myself * please don't try to talk her into stayin here, just let her fuckin go please, what the fuck is really goin on*

"Well I'm gone miss you girl.... have you said bye to Mommy and Daddy?"

"Yup, I did before I came over here. I made this my last stop before I hit the airport. I wanted to meet your dude but since he's so busy I guess I'll meet him another time."

"Oh well he's gonna get unbusy right now." I heard that and my heart almost exploded, I felt like having a panic attack. "Baby open the door just come say hi…. Please."

"Aight I be out in a minute let me finish this up, hol up."

I said tryin to think of a plan quick. I wasn't so sure that I would be able to get out of this one. If I didn't my life would mos def be over.

"Alright we gone be in the den waitin Bay."

"Yup" I didn't know what to do, I just figured I would stall time until she had no choose but to leave to catch her flight. I went to the door and peeked out to see where they were and sure enough they were sittin in the den on the couch waitin patiently for me to come in the room. I flopped back down in my chair and thought * Dammit … what the fuck have I gotten myself into … fuck it whatever it is it's about to be over wit tonight…. shit.* I shook my head in disgust and laid it on the desk. "hmm hmm hmm." I couldn't believe what was about to unfold.

After ten minutes had passed I picked up the phone and called Lloyd. "Whodis" he answered the phone almost soundin busy but I didn't care I needed to talk.

"Nigga you know who dis is, my number came up on yo shit."

"Whassup man you sound stressed."

"Nigga sound? I am stressed the fuck out … Dude why they both in the den!"

"Who?"

"Man please don't act stupid … dawg you know who."

"Dayum man you act like I did it shit … Ionno."

"Man Steph and Brina"

"You bullshittin, nigga I'm hangin up on yo ass."

"Nigga on erthang"

"how dat happen dude?"

"Man…." right in the middle of my sentence the door opened, I panicked instantly I felt the phone sliding from the palm of my hands due to the sweat that had formed immediately. I gripped it with all my might and began to pray *please don't let this phone fall* as I heard Stephanie's voice "Bay come on my sister has a plane to catch, she has to go soon." Without turnin around, scared to find Brina standin right behind her I thought to myself *bitch … how the fuck yo dumb ass gone leave the fuckin door unlocked!* I held my hand up as to tell her to lower her voice and then cover the phone and whispered "hol up Bay I'm on an important phone call."

I could tell she felt back cause she got that little hunch in her shoulders as to say oops and quietly said "Oh I'm sorry" and closed the door back softly.

Just as I had gotten excited thinking I had made it through the worst time of my life, the door came back open this time with Sabrina looking in right behind her. I glanced quickly to see what Stephanie wanted shocked to see Brina standing there this time, as soon as I seen her my heart began to race but I would not put down the phone.

"Well Bay she just want to say Bye." she said still whisperin. I threw my hand up and waved bye turnin my chair only slightly enough for her to get a side profile view of me. I covered the phone again as if the call was really important and whispered "sorry. I'm sure we'll meet again soon." I turned my back to them once again as I heard Brina respond softly "Oh I'm sure, yall be good. "the next thing I heard was the door shut behind them. I was relieved that it was over, I sat the phone down that seemed to have been glued to my ear and wiped the palms of my hands onto my lap. As soon as I got back on the phone Lloyd was crackin up laughin. "Yeah" I said letting him know that I was back.

"Nigga you sound suspicious…. How she didn't know it was you … yo scary ass."

"Fuck you bitch … shit I'm a pimp nigga … and she prolly didn't know cause I'm lounging, I got on a du-rag and a bath robe nigga she ain't neva seen me like dis."

"Nigga you the luckiest mu fucka I know, let that would have been me, it would have been game over dude" we both started laughin over the fact that he was right I got away wit shit that was practically unheard of.

"Yeah man I know right."

"That ain't cool Man…. You gone get it one day."

"Yeah Ok I hear you talkin but anyway let me get back atchu in a minute my dawg."

"Aight be easy pimpin … one."

"Yup" I hung up the phone surprised myself that I had actually gotten away wit such a close call.

I stood in the door listening to them say their goodbyes.

"So when will you be back." I heard Stephanie ask, my ears stretchin even harder to hear the response.

"Girl I don't know, but I do know that I want to see my niece or nephew born."

"Well that mean you have to come back in the next three months then huh?"

"Girl I will prolly be back here before then it just depends but if not yes that is what that means … and tell yo nigga don't be too busy next time … actin funny and shit … let her know I accept her for who she is."

As soon as I heard her say that I was sure she knew, I was anxious to know what Stephanie had said about me and how far their conversation actually went.

"Girl please, Fonzie is always wrapped up in his work, and I mean always, we never really have time for each other anymore. I try to tell him to slow down but I think this whole family things got'em shook."

"Steph … you can stop say in he now. It's out remember…. I know and I'm totally happy for you, all you have to worry about now is …"

"The folks" they both said at the same time and started to laugh.

"Girl I know I be forgetting but shit she straight … I mean well not straight …" Stephanie said with a chuckle and the quote end quote sign before she finished her sentence. "She's cool, just stay on the grind as she would put it."

"I understand completely." they hugged each other and I finally heard the front door close. I knew that Stephanie would make her back in the room with me to see what I was doin so I hurried back to my desk and sat back down pretendin to be on the web.

I heard the door open behind me but it was quiet. I refused to turn around, they might be tryna set me up. "Baby you cannot tell me you that you are that damn busy!" I could hear that Stephanie had an attitude from the tone in her voice, she didn't get mad often but when she did, it stung and she made sure you felt it. I spun my chair around to look her in the face, basically to see how angry she really was.

"What?"

"I don't appreciate you doin my sister like that Neko!"

"Doin yo sister like what, I told you early that I had a lot to do and I would be busy and that's that.!"

"Yeah Ok." Stephanie ended the conversation by slammin the door. I knew that Stephanie was mad but, not as mad as she would have been if I would have turned around and held a conversation wit her sister, so I accepted the anger and allowed her to slam the door wit out makin her come back and close it like she had some sense.

Interrupting my conversation my phone started to sing "Baby Baby Baby Baby Baaaabbbeee" that was Brina's ring tone. "Hello" I answered quick as hell knowin that the ring increases the longer the phone rings. * I never fuckin have my phone on ring in the house, I was slippin on my pimpin all around today* I tried to gather my thoughts so that I could talk on the phone.

"Baby I just called to tell you that I made it to the airport safe and on time."

"Oh Ok, so did you take care of the everything you needed to take care of?"

"Yeah and girl let me tell you ... well naw forget it I'll tell you later when you come home or I'll call you when I land."

"Quit playin you can tell me now. What happen?" I hate when she called me "girl like that, it made me feel all icky inside but, that was the game I played.

"It's nothing really, I was jus gone tell you about my sister's girl and how mean she is."

"Her girl? I thought she was pregnant."

"Exactly ... all this time I thought she was wit a dude but, I mean well really she is a dude shit she look jus like one and act jus like one so you know how that go. Walk like a duck and talk like a duck."

"Oh for real, you met her?"

"Naw I seen her rude ass though, she was too busy to meet me ... at least that's what she said ... I think she jus scared I'm gone call her ass out.... She must be hidin something, you know how sneaky Studs are."

"Yeah I do." I said takin the phone off my ear looking at it with disgust while she bad mouthed who she didn't know was me. "But you never know she might jus be busy as hell you know it gets like that sometimes. So but, other than that did she seem coo."

"I guess so yeah, she aight" she said as she stressed "aight" "I mean I jus don't get the whole tryna be hard role Studs be tryin to play. Do you?"

"I mean I don't get into all the labels I'm kind of over that a long time ago"

"Yeah I guess but, anyway my plane is boarding so I will talk to you later."

"Ok sweetie, I love you."

"I love you too"

CHAPTER 5

▼

IT'S A BOY

"Well from the looks of things … the way the baby is showing out, you're having a boy." A smile a mile away crawled across my face.

"I told dat ass!" I said as the Dr proceeded to take measurements of our son.

"So what nigga you are too geeked." Stephanie covered her mouth embarrassed that she had said the "N" word in front of our Native American Dr. "Oops I am so sorry." Stephanie apologized still showin her embarrassment.

"Oh honey you are Ok I've heard way worst." The Dr. responded. "Have you guys thought of any names yet since it seems you were already set on a boy?"

"Well I wasn't set on a boy that was her …" Stephanie said as she pointed to me. "So I'm assuming she has a name. So do you Fonzie?"

"Um well…." The Dr interrupted right before I could finish my statement.

"You guys are too cute, I have experienced so many different couples but, I have totally fallen in love with your love it is beautiful to see you two so happy…. You have truly changed my perception of well I mean …"

"We know what you mean and we thank you for not judging us, we don't get that a lot." I helped the Dr out a little it seemin that she didn't know how to choose her word correctly.

All day long after finding out we were havin a boy Stephanie kept comin to me wit dif'rent boy names. "What about Jordan Bay?"

"I don't really ..." I was interrupted by the ring of my phone. Stephanie huffed and bounced back on the couch and pouted her lips like a spoiled kid and mumbled "Here we go."

"What up doe" I picked up my phone but instead of me getting an answer I heard a bunch of screamin on my other end. "Oh my God ... Oh my God ..." the voice continued to scream. I instantly became frustrated with the caller and begin to scream right back "HELLO.... WHO IS DIS."

"NEKKKOOO ... NOOOOO.... NEKOOO HELP ME PLEASE HELP ME." the voice continued to scream, even though I couldn't figure out the frustrated voice I knew it had to have been somebody I knew personally cause they called me by my name.

"WHAT THE FUCK IS GOIN ON?" I asked getting irritated ready to hang up the phone.

"LLOYD, NEKO ... LLOYD GOT SHOT, I DON'T KNOW WHAT TO DO NEKO, THE DR SAID THEY WANT TO TALK TO THE IMMEDI-ATE FAMILY." the voice said crying on the other line, at this time I had figured out that this was one of Lloyd's female friends Jesse.

"OK hol up Ma calm down tell me what's goin on" I said tryin to get a clearer picture of the situation.

"they won't let me do any ... any ... anything, they want to talk to his family Neko." She finally caught her breath enough from crying to finish her statement. I was speechless all I could do was hold the phone.

"What's wrong Baby?" Stephanie asked being concerned by the look on my face. I held up my finger telling her to wait a minute while I tried to hear what was goin on in the background of the hospital. "So what are they saying" I finally said after gainin my composure.

"I don't know Neko but you gotta help me Neko I can't be wit out him ... I jus can't."

"aight look calm down Ma, I'm on the next flight out, where are you?"

"I'm still here at the hospital, I need to see him."

"Aight don't move Jess we on the way."

"Ok."

As soon as I hung up the phone, Stephanie knew it was something serious even though I had explained nothing to her, she started packin my bags for the flight out. She came out the room with my travel bag.

"Let's go Bay ... you can tell me on the way ... we need to get you to the air-port."

I loved Stephanie she knew how to react to all situations with no questions asked she had my back.

We drove to the airport as I told Stephanie what had happened to Lloyd.

"Bay, you might jus have to move to Atlanta to take care of things." she suggested but, I wasn't tryna hear that. If it wasn't one thing it was always something else.

"No I'm tired of leavin you like dis … I'm not movin no where shit what the fuck…. I'm gone see whats hatnin and I'll be back home." I said frustrated with jus the idea of havin to leave her at home alone and pregnant.

"Baby … I understand, this is your friend … me and the baby will be right here waitin for you when you come home, I promise you baby I love you."

"I love you too Ma."

After our conversation it assured me that she loved me unconditionally and I would never find anyone to love me like she did our shit was solid. It was time for me to sit back and reevaluate my life. This woman truly loved me and she lived in my world and only my world. Three was definitely a crowd. Reality was starting to bite me right in the ass.

CHAPTER 6

▼

THIS THING WE CALL LIFE

A couple of weeks had passed and I was still in Atlanta watchin over Lloyd as he made a speedy recovery. The doctors said that he made a miraculous turnaround seemin that he had been shot five times in his chest area. Someone was really tryin to off my man. The doctors had given him a clean bill of health and had decided to release him early with the hopes that he would continue his restrictions at home. I assured them that I would make sure that he would. "oh, you don't have to worry Doc he'll be straight, Ima make sure of that". I said reassuring her. "Well, I hope so we don't want Mr. Stevens back here talkin about something went wrong". We all started laughin, Lloyd tryin not as much, he wasn't fully recovered. "Don't be like dat Doc, I'm gone be good" Lloyd said holding his side as if he was in pain. "Alright you know I have grown on you or you on me, I want you to be fine". The doctor said I didn't know if she was being flirtatious but she was cute as hell, if I was Lloyd I would have ran with it and he did. "Yeah but not as fine as you" he counteracted. She smiled and walked out the door. "Um, cuse me Lloyd were you guys flirtin" Jesse asked, she had been there with Lloyd everyday too. That was his main girl, she and I bumped heads a lot even though she knew I had two different woman she hated me and Lloyd's relationship. I guess she thought I wanted him. "Naw", you know I love you girl" Lloyd said sarcastically. "Yeah OK" she said back while rolling her eyes. "Well nigga this is it, you bout to get outta here, man I know you can't wait. I got the guest room all tight fa you". I said, Jesse really started smackin her teeth and rollin her eyes, she was mad that he didn't want to go home and have her come to his house to take care of him but he just didn't want the disturbance. He knew that people would worry him to death of they knew he was home. "Yeah Man … I can't wait but uh do Brina know they releasing me today"? He said, squinting up his face like it pained him to talk. "Yeah she know and Jesse you know your welcomed whenever" I had to say that to make her feel special even though I know she didn't. "Thank You", she responded not sounding sincere at all. When they gone bring dat damn chair and my papers so I can get the fuck.…" and before Lloyd could get the rest of the words out of his mouth, his whole body started to jerk and he began to go into convulsions, it was like it was a movie. I went to grab him to try to control his body as Jesse screamed for the nurse. "OH MY FUCKIN GOD.… NURSE.… NURSE, SOMEBODY GET THE DR." she said screamin to the top of her lungs. It seemed like the whole hospital staff had mobbed the room. As they escorted us out I heard the doctor say "get him prepared for the surgery stat".

By the time the doctor came out of the operating room three hours had passed and Sabrina had made her way down to the hospital as well as a couple of more people Lloyd knew. I was on the phone with Stephanie explaining to her for the hundredth time what had happened as the doctor walked in "let me call you back here comes the doctor" I told her, "ok baby". I quickly hung up the phone before she could say I love you. I knew she wouldn't think much of it due to the matter at hand. "Um now who is Neko Jones" the operating doctor said, "That's me sir"

"ok, well I have to ask because you're his emergency contact. Do you want to step into the family room alone for a minute"?

"Well, everyone here is pretty much family so we can all go if that's o.k., we all wanna know his progress".

"That's fine" the doctor said as he showed us to the family room. The room seemed cold as hell and the doctor face was serious as we all sat there holding on to hope. "I'm sorry to have to tell this to you but there is no other way to say it" Jesse cut him off before he could finish, "just tell me that he's still here, anything else we can work through" she said with tears streamin down her face. "Well, unfortunately I can't say that". As soon as I heard unfortunately my heart hit the ground, my thoughts were scattered everywhere *not my nigga, what the fuck am I gone do now* Everybody started crying but Jesse had to be escorted out she was screamin so loud. No one could hear what else the doctor was saying. "Ms. Jones we tried everything we could, we had your brother in there for hours tryin to save his life, we just couldn't do it. After we finally stopped the internal bleeding his lungs collapsed … we tried, I am so sorry" the doctor said with the most sincerity. "I understand" I said with tears in my eyes. I thought to myself *why did this happen … what the fuck did he do to deserve this shit* Sabrina held me so tight.

"You gone be alright baby" she said.

"You think" I said back.

My emotions were runnin wild. I wanted Stephanie to be there with me so bad. That's who Lloyd liked the most anyway. He tolerated Sabrina but he knew that I was happiest with Stephanie. Sabrina just happened to be something to do then after a while she was hard to get rid of.

Goin in the room to see Lloyd for the last time was the hardest thing I had ever done. It seemed dark and cold. They had him layin on a cold steel table all cleaned up as if he was sleep with cover across his chest to his feet. I stood by him and talked out loud. "Man, this shit is crazy" I started cryin "I know a lot of people hated u fa getting money the way we did but damn nigga dis fa us … dis fa us … what the fuck am I gone do without you man". I wiped my face with my hand and held my head down. "I want you to wake up so bad man, don't you know this shit is killin me … I love you man and I'm gone miss you … man what the fuck nigga … man fuck it. I know what I gotta do, I just gotta be strong nigga and keep yo spirit alive nigga. Dats fa us nigga me and you. Fa my big brother man I love you dogg with erthang nigga. You be sweet nigga, I know you looking down on me now man". I kissed him on the cheek "one" before I left out the room I turned around and blew him one last kiss and exited the room. I told Sabrina to go home without me. I wanted to have time to myself. Of course she understood and she told me that Jesse was goin to come over as well, she didn't want her to be alone. As soon as I sat in my car I picked up my phone and spoke wifey into headset. That automatically dialed Stephanie's cell.

"Hey baby" she answered soundin so sweet but concerned.

"Bay" I started cryin.

"Don't tell me bay, please don't tell me he's gone" I shook my head before I could answer.

"Yeah, he gone baby" Stephanie started to cry.

"Oh no, bay I am so so sorry. I wish I could be there for you, to hold you. Bay I am on the next flight if you ask me"

"Naw baby, I am goin to have a small service for him her, I guess then I am goin to have one at home for his family and friends there so I will be home soon.

I know you wanna be here for me and I love you for that but I promise you I'm aight. You too far along in da pregnancy to be back and forth, you feel me"?

"Yeah Fonz, I hear you. Have you told his mom and his sisters"?

"Nope, I was hopin you would"

"Yeah bay I will, I will go by there right now. Hopefully I can catch somebody, you know how they are. But I will most definitely get the word out so people can prepare for his home going".

"Thank you baby, I love you"

"I love you too"

Once I hung up the phone I got to thinking about Lloyd and the relationship he had with his family, I had lost my mother when I was twenty four years old and I never had a relationship with my father. Lloyd on the other hand had a relationship with both his parents and his two sisters until one day his father had jumped on his mother and Lloyd pulled out a gun ready to kill dat nigga but his sisters stopped him, telling him that that was his father and he should forgive him. Ever since then Lloyd had cut his whole family off not understandin why his people allowed his father to treat his mother that way. He hadn't had physical contact with his people in three years but he still made sure they were set financially and I was left to make sure that would continue to happen. When me and Lloyd went into business together all of our paperwork consisted of me and him. Even insurance policies, if anything were to ever happen to him, everything would be left to me and vice versa. We only trusted each other and I knew what I was left to do.

Lloyd had passed away on Wednesday, July 17th. I had arranged for services to be held in Atlanta, Saturday July 20th and in Detroit, Sunday July 21st. I had already had the body flown to Detroit for preparation and there would be a closed casket in Atlanta. It was Friday and I got up to do some last minute running for the services. I still hadn't picked out the exact casket I wanted yet. Lloyd as picky and so was I. As I got up to leave, Sabrina was on the phone with what seemed to be an intense phone call, however I didn't read to much into it. I kissed her on the cheek and walked out of the door. Back in the house her conversation continued "That's sad Stephanie, I'm sorry to hear about your friend" Sabrina said thinking to herself *what a coincidence ... death is everywhere*

"Yeah I know ... you know you might've known him, he owned a Barbershop wit my fiancé Fonzie, he got killed there."

"Whaaat" Sabrina said. "What was his name, cause a friend of mine did just get killed here, he got a shop in da D too"

"Yup his name was Lloyd"

"Hell yeah that was my nigga, how did you know him ... through yo fiancé" Sabrina said sounding curious and startin to piece things together.

"Uh huh ... damn girl thus us a small world, I wonder if you know Fonzie den, there business partners, she is in Atlanta now makin the arrangements" Stephanie said sounding surprised however Sabrina was boiling inside but did not let Stephanie hear it in her voice, she knew now in her heart of hearts that Stephanie's Fonzie was her Nikola.

"I don't know Steph ... I might know her if I seen her but um ... well I don't know maybe I'll see her at the services."

"Oh yeah you will, she'll most definitely be there"

"Well I want to meet her and when I see her I'm gone tell her I'm your sister"

"Yeah you do dat and as soon as she come home Sunday for services here I'm gone ask alright ... I don't want to really talk about it to her now cause she goin through so much you know"

"Yeah I feel you" Sabrina said already contemplating on takin me down * dis bitch been playin me fa my sister all this fuckin time ... I don't know who the fuck she think she playin wit* she thought to herself.

"Well let me get off this phone Steph I gotta lot of shit to do."

"Alright then talk to you later sis"

"Yup" Sabrina had decided already not to get her sister involved in her madness until she knew for sure for her own eyes that Fonzie was indeed Nikola. She had a plan, a scant less plan.

Funeral services went as planned Saturday, the turnout was tremendous due to the short time Lloyd had lived in Atlanta. All of the frequent goers of the shop was there as well as friends he had met along the way. Sabrina was extra supportive, it's like she was in my body, she knew exactly what I needed. For a minute I didn't even miss talking to Stephanie.

As the night approached I began to feel overwhelmed knowing that I had a five o' five AM flight to Detroit, here is where I would have to face Lloyd's immediate family and all of the friends we grew up with. I lay across the bed looking up in the ceiling while Sabrina stood in the mirror.

"Do you love me Nik" she said starrin at her face looking for flaws.

"Of course, why would you ask"

"I just wanted to know ... I mean your friendship with Lloyd was beautiful and the things you said about him today were so ... I don't know touchin, I could see the genuine love … I hope if I were to go …" and before she could fin-ish I interrupted.

"Don't talk about that … I would never be able to cope if you left me" I said sincerely, even though circumstances were the way they were I had genuine care and concern for Sabrina, I truly loved her.

"Awe baby … do you mean that" Sabrina said out loud but in her head she thought *dis bitch is so fake, how could she feel that way about me and be com-mitted to my sister … oooh I hate dis bitch*

"Yeah I mean it … no matter what we go through or what I've done in the pass I love you … and I hate sometimes I do the things I do … I mean I try to correct things but some things take time … but regardless to what, Bay I love you and you remember that if nothing else, O.K."

"I will" Sabrina responded she thought to herself *maybe she do love me* I watched Sabrina comb her hair in the mirror as she sung the song from Lloyd's services "I need you now, oh lord I need you now, I need you right now, right now … I need you now" her voice was soothing.

"Baby can you hold me" I asked her, she put the comb down took a deep breath in front of the dresser turned around and responded.

"Of course".

Beep beep beep … the alarm clock sounded, it was three thirty in the morn-ing, it seemed like I had just closed my eyes. I wanted to turn over but I knew that I had to be well prepared for ten thirty a.m. in Detroit. I had snoozed the alarm so much that I only had time to wash my face and go. I left Sabrina sleepin so sound, she looked at peace so I left her a note *Baby I will be back sooner then u can miss me. Remember I love you no matter what* I made her a bowl of dry fruit loop with a half carafe of milk on ice so that she wouldn't have to get out of bed. Even though she didn't show it as much I know she loved Lloyd too.

My plane had been delayed an hour so by the time I landed in Detroit I only had time to take a shower and get dressed. Stephanie was definitely a sight for sore eyes. Her belly was protruding from a yellow summer dress which made her look as beautiful as the sun. Even though we were celebrating Lloyd's Homegoin we knew that he wouldn't want us to dress and act all gloomy. She wore some sandals that accented her feet, her toes and hands were perfectly painted to match the print in her dress. All I could do when I seen her was hug her so tight and start to cry, inhaling the scent of Donna Karen perfume. It definitely smelled like home.

"Baby everything will be fine, we will always have a part of him baby … I am carryin his child … our child"

"Yeah I know that's what keeps me sane bay … that's what keeps me sane".

"I can stand here all day and talk about my boy. We had so much together. Our love was beyond the limit. As you can tell even to the grave were alike" I said that referring to our attire, we both dressed in a tailor made Navy Blue suit with an orange button up, one button open at the top exposin the white tee, with the orange and blue gators to bring out the whole get up. Everyone slightly laughed.

"So at this point I am goin to open the floor to his closest friends and relatives, I would like to limit the comments to two minutes per person, thank you". And before I stepped away from the podium I looked over to Lloyd and said "I told u bouy … you thought I was gone crack didn't ya … haa ha … learn to believe in ya nigga, I told ya I got cha back … I love you bouy and you will truly be missed".

Everybody chuckled at the private conversation I held with Lloyd, it was like we were still bein silly even though he was gone.

Several people got up to speak on his behalf even his sister, she cleared her throat. "Um, I don't know where to start" everyone started to get emotional, especially his mother, she could not hold out. Her outburst "my baby … my baby … oh god I'm so sorry baby … momma is sorry, I swear to you I am". Her daughter said from the podium "I'll be o.k. ma" as her other daughter embraced her and rocked with her back and forth and listened to the speech. "My brother was sooo stubborn" she started to cry "When he said sumthin he meant it, when he was threw wit you he was threw. The last time I saw my brother was about two years ago when him and Fonzie opened the shop in Detroit. I went to the grand opening, me and my sister, he promised us that we would benefit from his wealth, he was the happiest he had ever been. He had briefly explained to us why he didn't come around anymore but he did tell us he loved us. That was the last hug, the last talk, the last smile, the last everything I saw from my brother …" she paused while still cryin "But we knew he loved mommy and daddy, he told us and showed us and we will always love you Pretty Boy with everything in our soul". Once she walked away from the podium the funeral home stood still. Then before I could close the floor a figure from the last row stood up and said "I would like to speak" I went to sit down as the lady walked towards the front. She was dressed in a black pants suit that looked like it cost a pretty penny. She was the outcast of the whole funeral, like she was up to sumthin. "My name is Destiny" her voice sounded familiar but you know Lloyd had so many girls who knew, it was easy to get them confused. "Me and Lloyd met about a year ago, a little over a year ago and um he was the man in my book … If I wouldn't have been tied up with someone else he would have mos def been mine. But we were just cool. I will miss his warmth and his lovin smile". she chuckled "And from the looks of this funeral home he will be missed by so many, he truly will be a legend in our eyes". She was right the funeral home was standing room only. As she walked from the podium she skimmed the room and her eyes landed on me through the veil. I felt a cold chill immediately. I shook it off and looked over my shoulder as she continued to switch back to her seat. I thought to myself *who da fuck is dat bitch … I gotta catch her after dis shit*

I stepped outside of the funeral home and began to look around the parkin lot to see if I could find the girl but I had no luck. As soon as I went to step into the back of the Bentley with Stephanie a hand tapped me on the shoulder.

"Excuse me, can I talk to you for a minute"?

I turned and looked and it was the girl, I quickly turned back to Steph and to the driver and said.

"Hol Up"

We walked back into the funeral home as she insisted and when the doors closed she revealed herself. My mouth dropped.

"Brina" I said shocked barely getting her name out.

"Yeah its me Fonzie, oops I mean Nikola".

"Look ma let me holla …" she interrupted.

"Ain't nothing to holla about, you played me … it's good though. I knew you wasn't shit but Ima tell you this … tell her or I will". She placed the hat back on and walked out.

I got back in the car and before the car could ride out Stephanie said.

"So who was that"?

Still dazed I responded,

"Um some girl Lloyd knew tryin to find out info about Jesse," I thought quick on the draw so she wouldn't be curious.

"Oh hell naw, bitches be killin me, so what I guess she wanna know who got what comin, huh" she shook her head.

"I'm glad me and you, are me and you"

I chuckled nervously and said.

"Yeah".

CHAPTER 7

▼

THAT'S WHAT FRIENDS ARE FOR

"Come on baby you can do it ... push ... push ... keep on pushin". Brina coached Stephanie on as the doctor watched on.

"I can't Sis", Stephanie started cryin.

"This is hurting meee".

"Come on Mrs. Jones you are goin to have to try ... push like you have to use the bathroom ... don't strain your face".

"I'm tryin" she said as she pushed harder.

After the incident at Lloyd's funeral prompted me to marry Stephanie as soon as possible, that next weekend I arranged a small ceremony for us. Sabrina seems to make her way into our life every chance she gets just cause she knows it aggravates me and has me on pins and needles. Although we married the death of my boy had me whiling out, I barely made it to the delivery of the baby. As soon as I walked in I was greeted by none other then Sabrina and Jesse.

"Glad you could make it" Sabrina said sarcastically, she wanted so bad to expose our relationship to Steph but she knew Steph would cut her off again and she didn't want to chance losin her sister all over ...

"Yeah", I responded.

"Waah Waah" the cries of the baby stopped all of us in our tracks. The attention was directed back to Stephanie.

"Oh my goodness he looks just like Lloyd baby ... look at lil Lloyd Jr."

"So that's what up ... his name is Lloyd" I said.

"Yeah bay we can't have it no other way"

"I love you girl"

"I love you too"

We all went home like one happy family. Me, Lil Lloyd and Stephanie oh, we can't forget Sabrina and Jesse. They had become permanent fixtures on the wall in our house. I really don't didn't complain cause they kept Stephanie busy. Everything was made to perfection when Stephanie walked into our room, she was exhausted so I tucked her into bed.

"Before I go pick up something to eat do anybody want something"?

Sabrina yelled, I knew she wasn't talkin to me so I didn't respond.

"No" Jesse and Stephanie said in unison.

"Good cause I'll be gone a minute ... um Fonzie try to act like you gotta fuckin baby now and sit yo ass at home" Sabrina said as she walked towards the door.

"Brina fuck you" I said tryin really to avoid confrontation.

Stephanie and the baby were sound asleep while me and Jesse finished up a half gone fifth of Absolute that we had just so happen to be drinkin on when Stephanie went into labor.

"I am so happy for yall" Jesse said.

"And LL look just like Lloyd don't he"?

"Yeah he do, my lil man is fine"

"Yes he is ..." Jesse took a deep breath "huuuuh....

I am so tired, today has been long and yo ass got me drinkin and shit, you know how dis shit have me nigga aint shit changed".

"Yeah well at least you wit da fam so you ain't gone be on no bullshit."

"Yeah aight Fam" Jesse said sarcastically, we both giggled.

"Why you say it like dat" I questioned her wonderin if I was jus buzzin and takin shit the wrong way.

"Like what" she squealed with a grin on her face.

"Like yeah aight fam." I said mockin Jesse.

"Ionno nigga it's jus that ... naw neva mind"

"What"

"Shit"

"Somethin"

"Nothin really."

"Aight"

We went back and forth for a minute and then the room grew silent for about five minutes. "Well it's getting late I'm bout to go to bed so uhhhh I will see you in the morning aight" I broke the silence.

"Aight" she responded back real quick bein caught off guard with me endin the night and as soon as I got up to walk out and go to my room Jesse spoke again "Fonzie" I turned around to look at her.

"What up?" she paused before she spoke again.

"nothing ... goodnight"

"goodnight"

All night I tossed and turned not bein able too really sleep, thinking about the conversation me and Jesse had and how we ended the night sleepin was out so I got up and went into the kitchen to fix me a bowl of ice cream. When things were heavy on my mind the only way I could keep from ponderin on it would be to eat so that's what I did.

I must have scared the shit out of Sabrina cause she almost jumped out of her panties when she walked into the kitchen about two minutes after me half asleep. I was sittin on the bar stool in the dark eatin my ice cream and sulking in what I was feelin for Jesse it was almost unreal, and the strange thing about it is that it seemed she was feelin the same way. Sabrina stumbled over my foot as it stuck out a little from under the isle, she jumped and held her heart "What the fuck are you doin up this late?" she asked still holdin her heart as if it would fall out if she let it go.

"Girl fuck you. Don't worry about what I'm doin up worry about you." This time I said it like I meant it, I could finally let out how I really felt about how she jus invaded our home and made my life miserable. Everybody was sleep and we were finally all alone, I didn't worry about her getting loud cause she knew the first person Stephanie would get mad at would be her if she was awakened besides this was our home and Sabrina was just a visitor.

"Fuck you you fuckin two timer, I fuckin hate your guts...." Sabrina said in a bitter tone as she rolled her eyes.

"Brina ..." I tried to calm her down a little bit cause I seen where the conversation was goin but she cut me off.

"Don't call me dat anymore ... my name is Sabrina that's what I would prefer to be called, you lost the privilege of callin me dat when what we had was over. We don't get down like that no more FONZIE!"

"Dayum Baby what's wrong, it's been months and you still mad. We should be better den dat Ma."

"You know what Fonzie you could have kept it real wit me, we had so much together, I really thought you loved me but what we had was all a game to you. Just apart of your lifestyle and that's fucked up."

"Yeah I coulda told you erthang but you would have left me just like you did anyway, I knew it was impossible to have both of yall for long g but I did what I did as long as I could. And no it wasn't a game to me I loved you and I'm sorry ... I still love you."

"No you don't"

"Yes I do ... I still look atchu and wanna fuck you real good, give you all of me and take all of you ... jus like now.... Can I fuck you real good?? Ain't nobody gotta know." I stood up off the stool and stood in front of Sabrina.

"Like you said ... I can't handle dat" she responded tryin to back away from me.

"Oh straight up ... you don't miss me? I can't suck on it?"

"Fa what Neko? So you can have me gone off you again? No thank you ... it's bad enough I have to watch you wit my sister being a happy little family." she shook her head in disgust "No fuckin thank you nigga."

"So you don't love me?" I said as I made my way in between her legs. She sat on the stool and tried to clinched her legs together but it was too late, I had made my way right where I wanted to be. She sat there tensed.

"You know I do" she said unable to control her emotions.

"So let me taste you." I kissed her neck, she shook her head no slowly and began to moan tryin to resist.

"No Fonzie, this ain't right." In between her telling me no I slide her pants down to her ankles and made my way down on my knees. I started caressin her clit with my tongue then kissin her pussy lips as if they could kiss me back allowing her juices to cover my face. She began to lift her butt from off the stool tryin to get away but I aggressively pulled her back down and entered my two fingers inside of her stayin in control and at the same time assuring her that what was happenin was OK. "Relax Baby ... I got you ... I love" I continued to let my fingers hit her spot and suck her clit.

"I love you too Fonzie ... oh my god I love you ... I have never stopped lovin you and I won't stop lovin you." she confessed her love to me as her legs began to get weak. Soon after she exploded I got up off of my knees with a smile on my face. I walked over to the sink with her wetness coverin my mouth and placed my hand under the hot water and threw it on my face.

"What was that for?" she jumped up from the stool and slid her pajama pants back up.

"Somethin for you to think about." I was bein cocky, I had gotten exactly what I wanted as usual. I looked at her with the desperate look of wantin to be with me in her eyes and smiled again before I walked out the kitchen into the den. "Goodnight" I told her, she just blew me a kiss and watched me as I walked away.

The cries of the baby had awaken me. I had finally fell to sleep in the den. I jumped up to go give him his bottle so that Stephanie could continue to rest. When I looked at the clock it was 3 o'clock in the morning. I looked over at Stephanie and she was still sound asleep looking beautiful as she always did. As soon as I got LL back to sleep, I kissed him then her on the cheek before I got up and moseyed back in to the den. I knew that I was goin to be unable to go back to sleep.

Jesse was laid across the couch watchin Friday after Next crackin up when I walked in to the room. I was thinking to myself *dayum can't nobody sleep tonight, shit this gone be a house full of zombies tomorrow. The only person that's gone be wide awoke is Stephanie.... And she still gone want a nigga to be bothered.*

"What you doin back up lady? "I asked her as I moved her leg over and flopped down on the couch next to her.

"The baby ... I heard him cryin and I got up to get him but you beat me to it.... Shit I came back in here to go to sleep but shit it was a DD ... I guess I got a lot on my mind."

"Oh Ok I hear dat."

We sat there and watched the movie as Jesse rolled up a peach white owl wit some purple. I hadn't smoked in so long but this night I wanted to get back to sleep.

"You gone hit dis shit?" she asked me wit her lungs still filled wit smoke.

"Yeah let me hit that shit" I reached for the smoke, she handed it to me and looked at me wit this look in her eyes.

"huh" she said handed me the blunt "but I wasn't talkin bout the blunt" she started laughin. As she was talkin I was inhalin the smoke and instantly started to choke shocked at her candidness.

"That's fa me huh?" is all I could say.

"If you want it to be sir."

"You trippen Jess ... you my nigga's girl."

"Yea but yo nigga is gone Neko and I don't want to be wit no other nigga. You da closest thing to him in my eyes you feel me? And I'm not tryna replace him wit you I jus wanna feel you dats it."

I was speechless, I started thinking to myself as I looked up to the ceilin * nigga let me know something.... Would you do it? Shit knowin yo freaky ass you would.* Jesse interrupted my thoughts by kissin me on my lips. It was a short innocent kiss but it meant something.... It lead to other things. I couldn't control my hormones any longer I had been thinking about her all night since earlier before bed. I strapped on and let Jesse ride me like I was a horse trainer. She was so wet the juices started to run down my thighs. She has total control and took the strap like it was the last time she would fuck in her life. I wanted to slap her ass but the noise would wake the house up. I grabbed that muthafucka tight as hell as she moved up and down bitin her bottom lip. "Take me" she leaned over and whispered in my ear. I wrapped my hand around the back of her neck and controlled the movement of her body, she relaxed her head back and placed her hands on my thighs and didn't care how loud she got. She moaned until she reached the point of excitement and exploded all over my strap. She collapsed on top of me and was tryna catch her breath. I looked up into the ceilin and thought to myself * Man please forgive me.... But dis was all for you. *

It was the middle of December; a couple of months after me and Jesse's first encounter but indeed not the last. We started fuckin like rabbits, there would be things she would do I had never had done. I had turned her into a real true freak. Every time we got together I would justify it as right by sayin "at least it's wit me and nobody else ... Lloyd would want it this way." I ended up jugglin all three women at the same time under the same roof most of the time in the same night.

Even though Christmas was around the corner (6days to be exact) I decided to go to Atlanta to check on the business there. Even though I had sold the other businesses and the property I had accumulated when I was livin there wit Sabrina, I still had the shop. I had been there in a while and plus I just needed to get away. I had promised Stephanie that I would be home before Christmas to celebrate for LL's first time. She was getting fed up wit me because I was becoming unreliable.

"Fonzie tell me the truth ... Will you be here or not I mean cause if you're not then we can go over my parents house and spend Christmas there."

"Baby I told you I'll be here aight." I said gettin irritated that she was questioning me.

"Shit what are you getting mad for Nek you're never here anymore Nek, it's always something more important than me and LL."

"That's not true Steph." I didn't want to argue but she kept edgin me on.

"Yes it is true Neko and I am sick of the shit ... I may as well be a single parent then to depend on you cause you don't give a fuck...."

"I DON'T WHAT?" I stood in front of her darin her to say another word. I was used to puttin my foot down and getting my way. What I say goes and if there was a problem in between that I would be quick to physically show her.

"Nothing Fonzie" she backed down "I'm just tired of this that's all. I don't feel like you love me anymore."

"Stephanie don't do dat.... I sick of the pity party you try to run on me it's always you feel like I'm this or that. I do love you if I didn't I'd be gone."

"You are gone Fonzie.... you're always gone.... I don't even know you anymore and I'm talkin about you ... NEKO JONES the person I fell in love with." she raised her voice in anger.

"LOWER YOUR MUTHA FUCKIN VOICE TALKIN TO ME STEPHANIE.... WHAT THE FUCK DO YOU WANT FROM ME STEPHANIE HUH??? I'M ONLY ONE PERSON SO WHAT DO YOU WANT??"

"I WANT YOU TO LOVE ME LIKE YOU USED TO DAMMIT. IS THAT TOO MUCH TO ASK FROM YOU!!!! IS IT FONZIE.... CAUSE YOU DAMN SURE AIN'T NEKO RIGHT NOW AND HAVEN'T BEEN FOR A LONG TIME!!!" she said sarcastically, I was tired of her patronizing me and callin me Fonzie the way she did. I took my backhand and with all of my might slapped her and made her neck jerk. Her eyes filled with tears as she held her face tryna stop her nose from bleedin.

"Now look I said I'll be back whether you be here or not when I get back, it's up to you." I calmed myself down and walked away leavin her standing there speechless sobbing.

CHAPTER 8

▼

LET ME BE ME

I touched down in Atlanta on a mission, tryna find the old me. I missed the way I used to be, not havin a real care in the world. Bein free to do whatever it was I pleased. I had one of the finest chics in Georgia runnin the shop. Her name was Dina, she was the only chic I had ever came in contact wit that I knew for a fact wouldn't let me hit it. We was cool as hell doe. She kept the bitches in line and the nigga's with the bread steady spending. She was about 5'9 brown skinned and thick as hell. Nigga's flocked to her like her pussy was platinum, shit they even had a rumor goin around dat when her pussy get wet it's like liquid diamonds. Whatever Dina wanted she got, sorta like my motto except she was a real challenge fa me but, my goal was to get it and it was rare that I missed out what I wanted if I put my mind to it.

My first stop was the shop, I think I walked in on the wrong topic ... nigga's and money. "If a nigga can't get me what I want den fuck'em.... Shit my pussy ain't fa free ... deez nigga's gotta pay royaly fa dis pussy." one of the customers commented.

"Girl I feel you shit half the nigga's be out here stuntin anyways. Like dey got it and ain't got shit. Fuck dey barely got a pot to piss in. All a nigga can do fa me fa real is eat my pussy and they can't even do that right half the time." One of the barbers said and all the girls roared with laughter and slappin hands.

"All yall need to leave dem hoe ass nigga's alone and holla at a real mutha fucka. Shit the dick is betta unattached anyway, you get the licky and the sticky at the same time ... have ya mind blown" I finally added in my two cents. They were shakin their heads up and down and laughin all at the same time. A couple of the girls were shakin their head in disbelief like they couldn't believe I had the audacity, I seen all kinds of reactions.

"Yeah you right, I would rather have a Stud any day then a hoe ass nigga ... that's what's poppin shawty." that comment started the crowd to continue to laugh.

"Where's Dina? Is she in the back?" I questioned changing the subject knowin that I was easily side tracked when it came to talkin to beautiful woman about convertin over to the other side.

"Yeah she in da back prolly watchin some ATL videos or sumthin." one of the girls said.

I walked to the back and kicked in the door real hard like the police scarin the shit outta her ass.

"Nigga don't be doin dat ol' gay ass shit the fuck wrong wit you?"

Nigga wit yo scary ass ... stop bein so noided what you got some pounds in dis bitch?"

"Not today nigga but dayum"

"Right if you did huh. You woulda been hit callin me like nigga come get me out dis mutha fucka I been knocked."

"Hell yeah pimpin you already know."

"So what's good Ma"

"Nuttin shawty but dis bread ya heard me. I'm throwin a gig up in da penthouse tomorrow so uh when you leavin to go back to the D?"

"Shit Ionno I jus got here today and shit so I prolly be here for a minute."

"Dats what's poppin pimpin, so you gone swing thru right?"

"Come on Ma you know if I'm in town it's goin down. Shit I gotta see how you runnin my shit you feel me? Plus you know it ain't a party wit out the star." we both started laughin.

"Yea ok shawty ain't nobody sayin all dat shit you looking at the illest right here pimpin."

"ha haaa ... I hear you talkin Ma. Ima get ready to get up outta here I got a couple spots to hit and uh I see you at the gig aight."

"Yeah aight pimpin."

"You make sure you be looking good fo a nigga like me"

"Whatever."

As I'm getting dressed for the party my phone rung. I started not to answer it cause my phone had been off da hook all day, everybody found out I was in town so they wanted to see me. I received so many messages askin if I was comin to the party it was crazy. I looked down at the caller ID and noticed the 313 area code-but didn't recognize the numbers that followed it. "Who dis" I answered curious to who was tryna get in touch wit me from da D.

"Nigga dis Black where da fuck you at out in dis muthafucka dawg … I den touched down and yo ass ain't nowhere to be found." I had totally forgot I had called her last night and told her to catch a flight out to dis party and I would meet her at the airport. I had gotten so fucked up the night before it had slipped my mind.

"Oh shit my bad dawg … where you at I'm about to send somebody?"

"Nigga I been here for two hours…. You thought I was gone wait at the fuckin airport fa yo forgetful ass … bitch I rented a car…. where u at?" We both started laughin.

"Fuck you dawg … I'm at da crib getting dressed."

The only crib I did keep in Atlanta was the first house me and Sabrina bought together. We both still had stuff there but we would never be there at the same time.

"aight nigga, I jus left the shop so I'll be dare in a minute."

"Who dare?"

"Nigga it's hoes shakin dey ass erwhere in dat muthafucka."

We both started singin "hoes in da club showin love shakin dat ass fa dat cash nigga whaat." and busted out in laughter.

"Aight den nigga I'll see you when you get here."

"Dat's what's up…. One."

"Yup"

We stepped into the shop and their was still a few people in the chairs getting dey hair cut I guess preparing to complete dey fit to go up to the penthouse. It was one hudred dollars a head to get in that was it kept all the small money niggas out.

"What up Fonz … dayum and BlackI ain't seen you in a minute yall looking good as hell."

"That's what we do Baby." Black responded to the barber.

"So where Dina at" I interrupted.

"She in da penthouse…. Shit the gig started at 8:30…. dis bitch was off da hook at 8. She den already kicked a bitch out fa slippin."

"Straight up … hahaaa dat's my dawg." Me and Black started laughin and givin each other daps.

We walked up the steps and as soon as the DeeJay seen y face enter the building he scratched the record in the middle of the song. Everybody started looking around like what the fuck is goin on including me I mos def didn't expect to get no special attention fa comin shit everybody knew who I was already I didn't need no grand intro. As soon as I went to say something to his ass the speakers started blaring "Meeeee aaannnd Mrs. Mrs. Jones. Mrs. Jones Mrs. Jones Mrs. Joooonnneess we gotta thinggg goooiiinnnn ooooonnnn." The biggest smile crawled across my face. I couldn't help but to blush it was crazy. They had actually planned a show fa me. They had a VIP area all pimped out wit Dom P at every table. The lay out was so fuckin outcold it had my mouth on da floor. I thought I do it big dey had me beat…. I guess everybody knew how much of a show off I was. Simone came from out of the floor in front of my chair wit a pink shear dress on outlined in stones wit some see through stilettos, her make up was flawless. I had never seen her look like she did that night … she was already gorgeous but this night Dayuuuuummmmm. She finished Mrs. Jones off by dancing for me. I guess she wanted to show me that she could have been one of the best dancers I had, which I never doubted that I jus didn't want her doin it. After Mrs. Jones went off she grabbed the microphone and seductively sung into it "I'd rather fuck you cause I love the way that you make me feeeelll…. I'd rather fuck youu ooo yeaaaahh yeaaahhh…." she took the microphone away from her mouth and placed it in front of me so that I could respond. I was still in shock that she was actually in front of me half naked in front of hundreds of people. I looked her in her eyes and sung back.

"Said I'd rather fuck wit yooooooouuu." I grabbed her by her waist line as she grinded in front of me. Everybody started laughin as I got more into it. I bit the bottom of my lip and continued to sing, "I'd rather fuck you cause I love the way you scream my naaammeee." I let go of her waste as she straddled my lap and the DeeJay started to play the original song. Simone had me in another world, I never thought that I could actually get horney off of letting somebody dance for me. Even though Simone had my attention I seen Black out the corner of my eyes tap one of the girls on the stage and motioned her down wit a stack of bread and then held her hands up in the air like "whats up" Ol' girl happily came down and obliged.

CHAPTER 9

▼

IS HOME WHERE MY HEART IS

It was New Years Eve and I had been spending everyday since the party wit Simone. She had kept my mind at ease, when I was wit her she made me feel as if I was the greatest person on the earth. How Stephanie used to make me feel before she became a naggin bitch. I still couldn't believe how she showed up at the party that night and pulled that dance stunt. She told me that Dina had called her at the last minute wit the plan to do it and she wouldn't have dared said no so she caught a flight that same day Dina called. She said she had been missin me anyway. To me that showed me that she truly loved me, she won me over completely that night. I took her home that night and fucked her real good and hadn't left her side since. I placed a block on my incoming calls and decided to take a break from my life in Detroit. That was something I truly needed.

It was around 11:56pm four minutes before the New Year in Detroit and I decided to call Black and wish her a happy new year. Me and Simone decided to bring the new year in laid up.... we celebrated on Detroit time cause that's where we really wanted to be so since we couldn't we pretended to be.

"Happy New Year my Dawg." I said before she could even get hello out.

"Same to you my nigga.... Shit what you got up?"

"Nothin man me and Monie jus chillen."

"Yeah that's what's up…. But look man I talked to Steph again today and I'm worried about her nigga…. I think you should call her I mean whatever it is you decide to do I think she deserve to know nigga she hurtin Dawg."

"Yeah I feel you but I jus don't know what to say."

"Nigga jus tell her the truth, stop makin her loose her mind Dawg she miss the shit out of you, she goin crazy Dawg fa real fa real."

"Word"

"Nigga hell yeah, I ain't neva seen nuttin like it, I told her if I hear from you den I would have you call her, she don't understand why you blockin her calls."

"Man I jus needed dis time dats all but Ima call her today matta fact Im about to call'er right now."

"Aight Dawg…. Happy New Year."

"Yup"

As soon as I hung up the phone my stomach felt sick, I felt bad that I had jus up and left Stephanie and LL wit no explanation but I needed a break I really did. I definitely didn't expect to come here and fall for Simone the wayI did. I shook the thought off and flipped my phone back open to call Stephanie and Simone stopped me.

"uhh uhh what are you about to do we have exactly 48 seconds for the new year you betta put dat damn phone down baby momma gotta wait." Simone reached to close the flip on my phone back down and before I could respond the TV started countin down 10…. 9…. 8…. 7…. 6…. 5…. 4…. 3…. 2…. 1 "Happy New Year Baby" Simone straddled me as she laid me back in the bed and kissed my lips. I wanted to be as happy as her and jus fuck da shit outta her right then but my conscious wouldn't let me. I was lost in thought. She tried to get me in the mood but I grabbed her by her waist and moved her off of me.

"What's wrong Neko" she said looking rejected "Aren't you happy ain't this what you want."

"Yeah I'm happy" I responded in a somber tone." I jus don't know if Stephanie is…. I need to call her and make sure she's aight."

"Alright den." Simone said climbing off of me and foldin her arms and poking her lips out like a big kid.

The phone rang three times before it was finally answered. "Hello" Stephanie answered sounding tired.

"Hay … Happy new Year" I tried to sound as if nothing was wrong knowin the sound of her voice was killin me.

"Neko?" she sounded surprised but still not enthused.

"Yeah dis me whassup Ma?"

"Nothin.... I guess you cared enough on the New year to call huh.... LL is fine by the way ... his first Christmas was great wit out his Nahne." she continued sarcastically.

"I'm sorry Stephanie, I had a lot on my plate."

"Oh and I don't? I had a fuckin baby for your ass that I have to care for all by my fuckin self Neko ... I bet you you're not alone are you.... I have been through so much with you.... I am so fuckin tired of bein hurt by you. I tried to be the woman you needed and wanted but nothing is never enough. You always searchin for something else. Why Neko?"

"I'm sorry Steph ... what can I do to make it up to you?"

"Fonzie" Stephanie paused and took a deep breathe "just tell me when you're coming home ... I want you to come home to your family ..." I could hear her cryin on the line. I knew that I could no longer lead her on. I wasn't happy anymore and I felt bad that we had a baby that was goin to suffer but I couldn't do it any more. I finally responded after I paused for a minute "I'm not."

CHAPTER 10

▼

STEPHANIE'S SIDE OF THE STORY

I hung up the phone from Neko and my world seemed to be over. I could not stop my tears from falling. *What is happening to me?* I thought to myself. I needed to talk to someone but Jesse and Sabrina went to a New Years Eve party. I wasn't in the mood to party, I just wanted to lay around and some how become invisible to the world. Me not talkin to Neko for those couple of weeks had taken a toll on me. There was one person I knew that I could call and get their undivided attention. I picked up my cell and scrolled down my phone book until I reached his name.

"Hello" the person answered on the other end of the phone.

"Hay how are you." I said still sniffing from crying.

"I'm good Baby how are you? You sound like you've been crying. Where's Neko?"

"That's why I'm calling you so late … I know it hasn't hit 12 o'clock there yet but …," the person interrupted.

"Oh yeah it is New Years there … Sweetie Happy New Years, what Neko went to a party wit out you as usual and left you there wit LL?"

"Somethin like that … but listen when are you coming back to Detroit?"

"As soon as I have my last procedure done…. It shouldn't be long the Dr said everything is everything…. Why?"

"Cause Bay ... Neko left me ..." I started to cry again this time even harder. "She left me and she said she wasn't coming back ... I need you to hurry up and come home, I need to see you."

"Whaaat!! Dat nigga did what? She den lost her mind. What the fuck is she going through? You know what don't even worry about it I'll be dare sooner den later to handle dat aight.... I promise."

"Ok ... please try to hurry I can't be here by myself ... I can't take being alone."

"Don't worry Bay I got you ... you know I do. You jus be easy Ma and I will see you soon."

Yeah, I'll try."

"Don't try do it bay.... How is LL?"

"He's good Bay ... he is getting so big."

"Yeah dat's what's up, I can't wait to see him ... look lay down and get some rest aight ... stop cryin erthang gone be aight girl ... I will see you real soon."

"Ok see you." I said before I hung up the phone. I needed to talk to him he assured me that life will go on without Neko. I layed on my back and looked into the ceiling and said a prayer outloud "Now I lay me down to sleep I pray to the lord my soul to keep if I should die before I wake I pray to the lord my soul to take ... god bless my sister, my parents, Jesse, my Baby, my special friend for his kind words and everyone else in my family ... Oh and God can you please make sure Neko burn in hell for making me feel this way? Amen."

CHAPTER 11

▼

SURVIVAL

I had almost survived a whole year without communicating with Neko. She would call me and I would refuse all of her calls. I wanted her to learn a lesson. She needed me and I knew she did. As much as I hated to I invited her to LL's birthday party seeming that it would be his first and after all Neko was his Nahne, she deserved that much. I mean she sent money and gifts all the time and inturn I would send pictures but she hadn't seen him since he was a baby, I wasn't ready to see her after she had hurt me the way she did. I decided it was time for me to stop being selfish and allow her to see him.

As soon as I heard her voice on the phone my heart skipped a thousand beats, I missed her sooo much.

"Hay Neko how are you" I said hesitantly not knowing how she would respond to hearing my voice.

"I'm good who'd is?"

"Oh forreal.... You don't know me anymore?"

"Oh what up doe Stephanie what's good witchu Ma ... shit I'm kinda shocked that you on my phone."

"Whatever Neko.... Anyway I was just calling to tell you about LL's birthday party next week.... I'm giving it at the house."

"Aight cool so what do he need? Well what do you want me to get him cause I know da lil nigga don't need shit?"

"Well I was hoping you would be here, it's his first birthday Fonzie."

"Oh so I'm invited? I mean well shit dat's whats up I will mos def be dare you know dat. Shit you know how you be you act like you can't be around a nigga...."

"Whatever Fonzie.... And yes I want YOU to come Fonzie.... Just you.... Nobody else." I made sure I stressed that point I did not want to have to face her girlfriend, I was still bitter over the fact that she left me for her after I had damn near allowed the bitch to be apart of our family. I allowed Neko to help her and her fucking nappy head ass kids.

"Oh hell naw what you mean ... my girl can't come?"

"Come on Fonzie you know the bitch can't come she is not allowed in my house ever again fuckin home wrecker ... besides I want this to be a good day for our son I don't want to regret inviting you.... Remember Neko this is LL's day."

"I mean I feel you ... so that mean yo partner ain't gone be there either right ... I mean fair is fair."

"I don't have a partner ... well not here anyway."

"Oh so whats that suppose to mean?" The tone in Neko's voice changed, you could tell that she was jealous to hear that I had moved on without her. "So you are seein somebody?"

"Look Neko just know that no one will be at the party for me.... I did not call you to discuss my personal life alright? We have both moved on that's for sure."

"You know what Stephanie I'm not tryna get in yo personal life I jus wanna know who you got around my son I mean shit is da bitch aight?"

"NEKO!!! I am not discussing my personal life with you Ok."

"Yeah aight jus send me a text wit the info so that I won't forget and I'll see you and my son then." You could tell that Neko was livid.

"Alright" I said before I hung up the phone. I held the phone up to my face and a big smile crawled across my face, it was good to know that she still cared with her jealous ass. * That nigga think she slick* I said to myself as I replayed our converstion back in my head.

All day long Jesse had been bragging about her new dude and how much we would like him when we meet him. She claimed he had a lot of money and was real down to earth. Sabrina and I was so tired of hearing LS this and LS that it was getting old fast. While we were setting up for the birthday party Jesse's phone rang she eased away from me and Brina to have some privacy. She walked back over towards us after she had hung up the phone grinning from ear to ear. "I hope yall don't get mad" she said unable to stop smiling.

"Mad about what?" Sabrina asked before I got a chance to.

"My man is outside, he said he wanted to see the birthday boy before the party started, he is crazy about kids.... Plus he wanted to meet yall before people started comin."

"Oh well girl if he's here let him in ain't nobody mad about that ... what would we be mad for?" I said waving my hand in the air at Jesse's stupid assumption.

"Shiiitttt I am.... I aint even dressed what the hell ... let me go put on some damn clothes." Sabrina said laughing as she walked towards the stairs to her room.

"Bitch please he don't care how you look ... he got a dime right here." Jesse commented sarcastically as she walked over to the door to open it.

"Both yall hoes crazy" I put my two cents in.

"Hay baby" Jesse greeted her friend with a hug. "Come in and meet my Family" she walked him all the way into the house, the house was a mess balloons were everywhere. As he made his way towards me balloons were hitting him in his head. He was very nice looking I had to admit.

"This is Steph.... LL's mommie." Jesse introduced me.

"What up doe Steph ... where's the birthday boy I heard he's fascinated with cars so I got'em something real special from his new uncle LS" He said as he held out his hand to shake mines.

"Hi.... Nice to meet you and LL is still sleeping I haven't woke him yet he has a big day ahead of him and I want him to stay up through the whole party.... You can give me the gift though and I'll put it on the gift table." I said trying to control my emotions, he was fine as hell, Jesse was right about everything she said about the nigga, I was totally amazed by his facial features.

"Oh well it's outside, we can't bring it in it probably won't fit on the gift table." After he said that I was thinking he had purchased LL one of those Tonka trucks that I see the little kids in my sub division driving up and down their drive ways, I instantly got excited cause I had said that I was going to get him one when I thought he was big enough. We all rushed to the door to see what he had gotten and sitting in my garage with a big navy blue ribbon on top of it was a 1967 Cadillac Deville sittin on 22" chrome wheels, the whole fuckin car was outlined in Chrome. My mouth dropped to the floor I was speechless, I looked over at Jesse to find that she was looking just as shocked as I was. I can see Jesse punch LS in the arm from out the corner of my eyes. She gave him a look of disbelief, like she was disappointed in him. I screamed in the house for Sabrina to come down the stairs.

"Brinnnnaaaaa come here bitch … come and look at what Jesse's friend bought my baby."

Brina came down the steps as fast as she could, you could smell her Victoria Secrets body spray lingering behind her as she made her way to the door. She looked at the ride then back at him, at the ride then back at him again. I could tell that she was about to say something off the wall cause that's just how Sabrina is she has always been the blunt sister. "Daaayyuuumm Mr nice to meet you by the way here is a fuckin expensive ass car for a lil boy I don't even know ass nigga." She grimmed him up and down again while we all bust out in laughter.

"Brina dis is LS" Jesse introduced them "LS this is Brina you know the crazy one I told you about." She gave him a strange look.

"What up Brina Brin" he said as he held out his hand to dap her up.

"Naw the question is whats up witchu Mr L to the mutha fucken S…. what does that stand foe Long Stacks?" Brina bust out laughing at her own joke.

"Naw but shit that's a good one I neva heard dat but it stands fa Lil Soldia…. They used to call me LSB fa Lil Soldia Boy but I dropped the B when it was evident that I was a grown ass man Now it's Uncle LS."

"Oh aight Uncle LS so um what made you buy my nephew a car like dat I mean shit you come in here actin like you Fam forreal."

"I am Fam if Jesse Fam, dis my girl and she told me that Lil Man love cars…. so dis how we do in my Fam. We do it big no doubt."

"I mean I feel you but…."

Jesse interrupted Sabrina And LS' conversation as if it was getting too personal.

"I hate to break this up but Bay come to the patio so that I can start the grill." Jesse looked at Sabrina and rolled her eyes as she grabbed LS' hand and walked him towards the back door to the patio.

"I don't care about getting no funky ass attitude shit I wanna know what's really good wit dis nigga." Brina said as Jesse slammed the door behind her and LS.

"Girl you silly … he straight ain't nothing wrong with that man." I commented.

"Bitch please … I'm forreal next thing you know LL gone come up missin and shit…. He gone been den snatched my nephew up and changed his name to LSB" we both started laughing.

"Girl shut the fuck up"

"Forreal Stephanie when it come to shit like dat I be havin my eyes on a nigga shit I'm like Nino Brown from New Jack City.... Brina don't trust a muthafucka" she said interpreting the character from the movie she had me crackin up. We continued to laugh and talk as we put the rest of the party streamers up.

It was a couple of hours into the party and everybody seemed to have been enjoying themselves. So many people had showed up it was almost unbearable, I wouldn't have been able to do it without Brina and Jesse they were definitely angels sent from above. They seemed to have been enjoying the festivities more than the kids.

Me and LS had finally had a minute alone, it was hard being in the same area as him and not being able to hold him. I had given him the biggest tightest hug I could muster while looking out the kitchen window into the backyard to make sure we were safe.

"When did you get here and why haven't you called me?" I questioned him.

"I've been here for a while ... I wanted to call you but I seen Jesse over my peoples house and one thing led to another and well you know how that go ... I'm sorry Ma ... I didn't...." before he could finish I interrupted I was just happy to see him it had been so long.

"Sorry for what? You don't have to apologize to me I understand. I am just so damn happy to see you and hold you ... I needed you to be here you don't understand when I seen you I couldn't believe it was you she was seeing. I almost couldn't hold in my emotions I wanted to grab you and hold you and kiss you...." I continued to ramble I wanted to get everything out I had to say before we were interrupted "I mean so she knows? I mean well do you plan on telling her about us?" I needed to know how much he cared about me I needed to know where we stood.

"Hell Naw I'm not telling her about us, not right now anyway. I love her and she loves me, I can't see me hurting hurt like that."

"So what about us?"

Before he could answer the question I seen Jesse walking towards the patio with none other than Neko, she always found away to ruin shit.

"SHIT!" I said outloud smacking my lips and backing away from LS.

"What" LS turned around to face the door as Jesse walked in with Neko.

"What's good people" Neko said with her vain attitude.

"Hay" I responded.

"So I see the birthday boy is enjoyin the festivities, he den got so big ... sorry I'm late, my plane left late".

"Oh, dats o.k., I figured you would have some type of excuse" I retaliated.

"Oh yeah ... dats fa me Steph" I rolled my eyes before I responded.

"Yeah dats fa yo sorry ass" I had to admit seein her brought all of the bitterness out of me. I wanted to slap her where she stood.

"Dayum, it seems to be tension in the air" LS joined into out battling conversation.

"This ain't nuthn new bay ... LS dis is Neko ... Neko this is my man LS" Jesse introduced the two as I continued to roll my eyes.

"So dis is Neko, what up dawg, I den heard a lot about you ... and I gotta admitt, I'm a lil envious ... your family is beautiful ... one day I wanna be just like you".

"Oh yeah ... shit the way dey treat me around here, I don't even wanna be me" they both started laughin and slappin hands. My face was as serious as it was when Neko first walked in.

"Whatever Fonzie, you brought this treatment on yourself" I said as I walked toward the door to go outside.

"Steph can we get along ... at least for the day" she commented back to me.

"Yeah whatever" I rolled my eyes and walked onto the patio.

I was beginnin to get frustrated with the relationship between Jesse and LS. They were spending days together, she had even moved her stuff out of the house. LS would still come and visit me frequently but not as much as he should I thought. I tried to convince him into telling Jesse that I knew everything and that he wanted to be with me. However, he told me that that wasn't a good idea because it would spoil everything. I began to start believing that LS just wanted his cake and eat it too. I mean or maybe I was just being paranoid. He was doin everything he said he would do. He had even befriended Neko as planned and he was getting to know LL more and more everyday, which was good besides this was the man I wanted him to call daddy one day.

Neko and LS had become hangin buddies. They had became so close, LS would fly back and forth from the "D" to the "ATL" all of the time. They were even talkin about goin into business together. LS kept me up to part on all of the their dealings together. He had told me that Neko was planning to sell Lloyd's share of the business to the highest bidder. See since all of the policies, Lloyd had made Neko the beneficiary, she was in control of what went on with his portion of the business and Neko claimed to be dealing with Jesse and feeling obligated to take care of her so she figured of she sold Lloyd's share of the business she could give his family the money and wash her hands with the whole financial issue. I thought it was a bad idea for LS to even consider bein partners with Neko considering our plans, so I told him to talk Neko into a settlement agreement with the family and to have Lloyd's name removed from the business altogether. It was late and I had just laid LL down for bed, Sabrina was in Las Vegas and I was preparing my foot spa so that I could relax my feet and watch a movie. Unexpectedly the doorbell rung.

"Who is it" I asked sounding irritated. I was mad as hell that I decided to go without having a butler, me being the all american woman and still ended up alone half the time.

"It's me Bay, open the door" LS responded from the other side of the door sounding just as mad. I hurried and opended the door anxious to know what had him in an uproar.

"What's wrong wit u Bay" I asked curiously.

"Man, what the fuck ... you wasn't gone tell me bout Neko and Jesse"?

"Tell you what ... what about Jesse Neko and Jesse" I asked sounding surprised dreading tohear what was next.

"So you telling me you ain't know dey was fuckin"?

My heart dropped as much as I wanted to be over Neko it still hurt to heat shit she had done to me, it got worse and worst.

"Naw I ain't know that ... are you serious ... who told you dat ... I mean ... well ... when, how"?

LS went to sit on the couch to explain, "Man me and Neko just left the bar talkin about what you told me to tell him to do about the hook up and you know we jus got to kickin it and she told me about yal as if I didn't know and she told me about her and Brina which didn't surprise me cause I'm the one who told you den she turned around and told me about Jesse, man I couldn't believe dat shit. I felt like throwin up right dare bay.

"Why ... why did you feel sick, I thought yal were over"?

"Bay still ... don't tell me it don't fuck you up too"?

"You know LS all the shit she has done to me nothing surprises me anymore ... I mean shit I remember when you told me about her and Brina, that shit cut like a knife but I still didn't leave her. Knowin they probly was still fuckin and I neva brought the shit up to neither one of them. I let it go, you know, I just want this shit to be done wit really. I'm ready to live our life Bay, me and you ... fuck dem".

"Yeah I hear you man but damn this put a spin on da plan cause now ... well fuck it, we'll work it out".

"Yeah we will but now you need to be sayin fuck Jesse and telling her about us.

CHAPTER 12

▼

IS THAT THE END

For some reason Neko had been on my mind for the whole day. I know that she had flew in from Atlanta a couple of weeks ago but we had not talked at all. LS was my only way of knowin what was up with her and lately he had been keeping quiet when it came to her. I figured things were ok. I was in the kitchen makin LL's organic meals when my cell phone rang *What goes around … comes around … what goes up must come down. Now whos cryin, desiring to come back to me* once I heard the ringtone I knew who it was immediately. I smiled and rocked to the beat of the song, for a minute before I answered it. I still get that feelin in my bones when I would hear from her.

"What's up" I answered the phone.

"Hay Steph, u busy"?

"Nope, why"?

"Shit, I wanna come see Lil man before I fly out. Yal been on my brain all day. I need to see yal, it's been a minute".

I looked at the clock over the stove to check the time and make sure she had enough time to get the the house and be gone before LS would come over.

"That's crazy, I've been thinking about you all day too … what time you leavin"?

"My flight leave at 4:25 a.m., why what time is your man or woman or who-ever comin thru"? I smacked my lips, "You ask too many questions … look it's almost 7:00, you know LL get put down at 9:00 and my man will probly be callin me around 10:30, 11:00 so you don't have to much time".

"Oh yeah ... yo man huh"

"Bye Fonzie"

"Yeah aight".

As I was getting ready for Fonzie to come over Sabrina walked in the house talkin shit, "Dayum a bitch must be bout to have company ... she looking good ... smellin good" she grabbed my shirt to expose what I had on underneath it.

"Yup and she got her T-shirt wit no panties on ... let ne get my over night bag and get the fuck out like I just came in, it's about to be some hanky panky goin on" we both started laughin.

"Shut up Brina, you don't know what you talkin bout"

"Shiiit who's the lucky winner"?

"Nobody fool, Neko comin to see LL before she go home". Ssbrina's face instantly turned up and her eyes rolled so far in the back of her head I was afraid they wouldn't straighten back out.

"Oh, that loser ... well you right ... she's not a winner at all"

She said sarcastically.

"But I'm still gone go cause I know yo weak ass, you been waitin for the moment to be vulnerable again for that snake".

"Whatever" I retaliated. Regardless to what anybody said about Neko I was still hopelessly in love with her and I knew if she would have me back I would oblige in a heartbeat however she had moved on and in order for me to get over her I had to move on too.

I opened the door and there she stood looking good as usual. Wit her navy blue and white durag and navy blue New York baseball cap. Navy blue T-shirt wit some blue jean Girbauds saggin just right. As soon as she walked into the vestibule she removed her Timberlands and gave me a hug. Just like she used to. I didn't want to let go. I inhaled the scent of her Jean Paul cologne as if it was new to my nose. I quickly gained my composure.

"LL in his room watchin Spongebob" I said.

"Don't he get tired of Spongebob"?

"Nope ... not at all" I said following her as she made her way back to his room. I watched her pick him up and hug him so tight. He was happy to see her as she was him.

"Nahnie" LL said excited to see Neko, that wasthe name LL gave her.

"What's up Nahne's lil man … you watchin Spongebob"? LL shook his head and pointed at the T.V.

"Well Nahne bout to go back home and I wanted to come see my lil man before I left and tell you love you … Kay" LL shook his head and said.

"Kay"

"Give me hug … hug Nahne neck" As LL went to hug Neko's neck I seen a tear form in her eye. It made me start to cry too. I knew she missed us but for whatever reason she couldn't stay wit us. It wasn't up to me to figure out anymore, we were over. I left her and LL alone and went into my bedroom to watch T.V. As soon as I sat on the edge of my bed my phone began to ring. *caught up got me feelin it…. Caught up … * I answered it quickly knowing that it was LS, he was calling early.

"Hay Baby" I was excited to hear his voice.

"What's up Miss Lady?"

"Nothing … missing you."

I miss you too."

"So are you coming over Baby."

"I wish I could but I'm still in Atlanta, I think I'm gone be here for a few more days…. but look I might need you to do something for me tomorrow."

I smacked my lips with dissapointment "What L?" he could hear the frustration in my voice.

"I'll talk to you about it tomorrow but right now I'm makin a few moves aight?"

"Yeah Ok" I was so hurt I wanted him to be home with me.

"Hay…. don't be mad I'll be there sooner than you can miss me."

"That's impossible I already miss you."

"Baby you makin me feel bad … don't do dat."

"Alright I'll talk to you tomorrow."

"Aight"

I hung up the phone and bounced my head back hard onto the bed.

"That musta been your date canceling on you huh?" Neko said startling me. I jumped up and looked at her with my disgusted look.

"How long have you been at my door?"

"Long enough to hear you have a attitude cause a nigga ain't comin to see you."

"Fuck you Neko … you can lock my door on your way out … what is LL doing?"

"Layin in his bed goin to sleep.... Oh so you can't walk me out? We like dat cause yo hoe ass friend stood you up?"

Neko said as she walked over and sat on the edge of my bed.

"No cause I'm mad and it don't have nothing to do with being stood up" I pouted my lips and folded my arms.

"Don't be mad … don't eva let nobody get you mad you hear me?" Neko said as she crawled up in the bed nest to me and put her hand on my thigh. I wanted to bust a nut right then with just one touch from her. She had the hairs on my neck standing straight up. I hadn't felt her in so long my whole body was numb. She kissed my neck and then my face and even though my mouth wanted to say no my pussy was screaming suck it, fuck it, get it how you live. She lifted my tank top up over my breast and my nipples were already standing at attention. She caressed them ever so gently with her tongue, softly teasing them with her teeth. My pussy contracted getting even more wet with each movement she made with her tongue. She started telling me how much she missed my pussy as she made her way down to my thighs. I wanted to make her stop because everything in me was telling me that this wasn't going to last but her tongue finally hit the spot. It touched my clit. My body went crazy. I was missing her and everything about her especially how she made me feel and with every stroke of her tongue and new trick she had up her sleeve I could tell she was missing me too.

I let Neko sleep until 3 o' clock in the morning before I woke her to catch her flight. Just like old times she was up and in the shower while I cooked her breakfast. When she was finished getting dressed her breakfast was waiting on the table and as always I prepared her a briefcase with some magazines to read on the plane and some peaches and cream werthers originals hard candy.

"So how long will you stay away this time" I asked her with my hands on my hips watching her eat her bacon. I loved to watch her eat bacon. For some reason it turned me on…. maybe it was the way she caressed the meat.

"Not long … I'm thinking about comin back … I miss my family."

"Yeah right Neko … you don't miss us."

"I do Steph … I miss da shit outta yall … I love you."

As Neko talked my mind wandered on all the things we used to doand how my life ahd changed. I wanted her to come home so bad I wanted things to back the way they used to be but I didn't know if it was too late. I had made a commitment to someone else who I wasn't sure loved me the way Neko did cause even though Neko fucked over me I knew in my heart of hearts she loved the hell out of me.

"Well if you decide to come back Neko you know I'll be waiting but if not then good luck" I was unsure if I should have even let that come out of my mouth. I didn't want her to take advantage my feelings.

"Yeah aight Stephanie ... you jus remember that I love you and don't forget that for nothing in this world. My life has not been the same without you. I don't breathe the same anymore. You and LL is my love and we will be a family again one day I promise you dat.... kiss my little man for me and you be good." Neko began to walk out the door and her words were still going through my head in slow motion.

"I love you too" my words lingered through the air as she walked down the walkway.

For some reason Neko's last words kept lingering in my mind. They were so real, she poured her heart out to me and really that was the very first time that I can say it was said with the most sincerity. I wanted her to come home but something was telling me it was too late. I knew that right now as we speak LS was trying to find a way to have her dealt with for hurting me the way she did. He had told Jesse in an earlier conversation that he wanted her to be the one to do it and of course she was game cause she thought it would benefit her and LS' relationship. He had her believing that once he had gotten the job done they would own all of his shit and he would make her wifey. The reality of it was after the job was he was setting her up to take the fall so that we wouldn't have any problems getting married. At first the idea was gravy. I didn't like how Neko was pkaying me she was heartless in my mind and I wanted nothing more but to get revenge. I wanted her gone so that she wouldn't be able to do this to anyone else. But after last night my mind had changed, I loved her.

I picked up my phone and spoke LS into my handset.

"What up doe" he answered sounding more hyper than usual.

"Hay bay what are you doing?"

"Shit chillen what up my nigga" I took the phone away from my ear and looked at it with confusion, he was talking to me like I was one of his boys right then I knew something was up.... he must have been around someone who wasn't suppose to know he was talking to me.

"Bay why didn't you call me last night.... I have been thinking hard about this and really I don't...." before I could finish my sentence he interrupted me.

"Yeah dat's what I'm doin right now Me and Jesse pickin out her ring as we speak so uhhh jus get yo shit tight cause when we get dis weekend it's gone be some nuptials dawg." My heart started pounding I didn't know whether to be excited or mad, all I knew is I was shocked. I held the phone long after LS had hung up I couldn't help but to feel bad for Neko * dammit Neko why did you have to be such a fucking player…. I am mad at you…. now this nigga is ready to kill you. Shit I shouldn't have been with this nigga anyways, he was of limits from jump* I shrugged my shoulders as I put the end of the phones atenna in my mouth and continued with my deep thought. *Shit it was Neko's fault I even start dealing with the nigga in the first plae so why am I feeling so bad? Shit she would probably have done the same thing to me fuck it.*

It was Tuesday and I hadn't heard from LS since Sunday when he told me to prepare for our wedding. I watched the news everyday to make sure there was no breaking stories. My insides were nervous, I didn't know what was going on. All I knew was that the shit was starting to freak me completely out. I wasn't cut out for this besides I didn't think it was such a good idea after all. I still hadn't found my dress bu with Sabrina's help everything was all set for Saturday at 6 o' clock. She was still in sibelief and so was I sort of.

"Girl I can't believe you bout to marry dis nigga…. you don't think that's wrong?" She questioned me for the hundredth time.

"Nope … that's my baby daddy." I started laughing.

"uww bitch you is so wrong."

I had told Sabrina the whole story from the beginning to the end. From how me and LS started talking to why I kept it a secret for so long. We sat up almost the whole night talking about it.

"Why am I wrong?"

Sabrina shook her head like she couldn't believe that I was asking her that question before she finally answered.

"Cause bitch he was off limits Neko is his friend and what about Jesse?"

"Fuck Jesse shit…. she said fuck me and shit from what I heard she had a problem with me and Neko anyways so she deserve whatever." I had left out the fact that LS was going to have Neko killed for what she had did to me. I knew if I would have that she would be furious.

"What about Neko, what you think she gone say when she find out you and her …" she held up the quote end quote sign up "… dawgs master plan."

I shrugged my shoulders "You know what I don't know I haven't thought that far" I lied, I thought about it everyday and I prayed that my conscious would leave me alone.

"mmm mmm mmm giirrrll you scatless…. my sister adirty bitch." We both started laughing.

"Fuck you Brina."

"But you kno what I think I like it shit I ain't mad atchu, I'm happy for you As much as Neko fucked over you you need to shit in her face let her see what it feel like. Shit don't hate da player."

"That's right bitch whats Neko's favorite line don't hate me cause you ain't me."

We clapped hands and started laughing.

CHAPTER 13

▼

I woke up to Sabrina running into my room screaming "turn on the TV oh my god turn on the news … what the fuck Stephanie turn on the news." She was screaming and crying out of control, she could barely catch her breathe. I jumped an turned on the news and as soon as I turned to channel 14 two pictures were plastered across the screen. One read Neko Jones and the other read Jessica Vasquez. I couldn't gather my thoughts, tears began to fill my eyes as I heard the report. Sabrina sat on the edge of my bed holding her face looking as if she was going to collapse.

"Home invasion has claimed two lives leaving one in critical condition. Officials say they are trying to positively identify the one of the victims who is said to be a black male in his early 30's identification was not on his person. Right now they are not releasing anymore information regarding the victims as the investigation continues they have no motive and no suspects. Well have more on this story and more at 6." I turned the TV off and just began to rock back and forth. My whole body was shaking, I was wondering what went wrong…. who was alive and who was dead. All I could do was wait and cry. I couldn't believe that this was real I wanted this to be a bad dream. Sabrina scooted over next to me and gave me the tightest hug all I could do was let out the biggest cry I had ever cried for all the pain I was feeling just then. "NOOOOOOOOO"

"It'll be OK sis" Sabrina began to rock me back and forth.

"Why is this happening to meee pleasssssseeee goooddd help meeee." I cried, I was so loud I ended up waking LL out of his sleep. He came running in the room to see what was going on.

"Mommie Kay" he said pointing at me recognizing that I was sad and crying. I picked him up and just held him. "What have your Mommie done L? What has your Mommie done?"

All day I sat in a daze in front of the T.V. listening to every report possible on every single news channel. I still hadn't heard from LS so I was hurting worst. My life was over. I had found out by listening to the news that the only one survivor was Neko she was in critical condition with a 10 % chance of survival. My heart went out to her. It was because of my stupidity that she was there. She always talked about not wanting to leave the world by someone taking her life. She wanted to grow old with me and LL. Jesse was shot 2 times in the head execution style she was pronounced dead at the scene and the third person was shot in the face neck and head and had still been unidentified. I prayed that the third person was not LS. My thought was him and Neko got into a shoot out and both ended up hurt. I refused to move from in front of the TV until I found out wh the third person was. It was eating me alive. The phone had been ringing all day but I couldn't bring myself to answer it afraid of more bad news. Plus I knew that people wanted to bother me with a thousand questions and wondering if I was OK but, of course I wasn't. It seemed like everything went wrong. I was in a state of shock.

"Caught up got me feelin it ... caught up...." as soon as I heard that ringtone my heart damn near stopped. I dove over my bed for the first time that day and grabbed the phone off of my nightstand. I prayed it was LS and not one of his boys telling me that he was third person found dead.
"Baby" I said sounding unsure.
"Hay Ma ... you OK" the sound of his voice was overwhelming all I could do was cry.
"Baaaabbby, no are you OK ... whats going on ... where are you Baby ... I miss you ... I'm so glad to hear your voice oh my goodness you just don't know."
"No trust me I do ... so look I'm in the D so I be atcho crib in about 10 minutes aight."
"A;right"
"A"
"huh"
"You ready for Saturday right?'
I took a deep breathe before I finally answered "Yeah Baby I'm ready."

We hung up the phoenand my heart felt so much better. LS was still alive and Neko was hanging in there. I mean I felt relieved even though Neko was suffering. That's all I wanted for her anyway, I didn't want her to die. I looked up in the sky and asked * God I know I said let Neko burn in hell but … is it too late to take it back … I mean I forgive her.*

While Jesse's family celebrated her homegoing I was marrying the man that she always thought would be hers. My thoughts of her didn't go unnoticed, I hated that she left the way she did but, that was truly out of my control.

All day I had prepared myself for the big moment. In a weeks time everything had been put together perfectly. As if we took years to plan it. Sabrina was my maid of honor and of course LL was LS' bestman. It was almost the most beautiful thing I had ever experienced. Loving Neko was the first. Our family and friends filled the church on both sides which held over 250 people. They all watched in disbelief, who would have actually thought that we would end up being together.

We stood at the alter as we recited our very traditional vowels.
"I do" I said with a smile on my face.
"I know pronounce you husband and wife Mr. Lloyd Stevens I know you've waited long for this so go ahead and kiss your bride." That kiss was the longest most sensual kiss I had felt in a long time from a man. I wanted us to work. The decision I had made was final and there was no turning back.

After the ceremony was over Lloyd had something up his sleeve before we went to the reception hall. Even I didn't know what it was when he ordered the driver to stop at Henryford Hospital. I looked at him with confusion on my face. I knew that Neko's family had her flown here from Atlanta so that they could be closer to her in her last days but I was still unsure of what Lloyd was up to.

My nerves were all over the place when we walked into the hospital. We walked ove rto the desk and asked to see her but she had so many visitors on a daily basis her family had to make a list of close family and friends only. It was so bad that she even had police security standing outside of her room. I had never seen anything like it.
"I am Stephanie Stevens…. well I would be on the list as Stephanie Owens but I just got married today …" Iflashed my wedding ring at the receptionist as if

the wedding attire wasn't good enough "and well me and my husband would like to see her."

We knew that I would be on the list but Lloyd uhh no, besides he was suppose to be dead. The receptionist looked up my name and finally said "Oh OK here you are Ms. Owens...." she paused as she continued to look on the list "and who are you Sr?" she questioned Lloyd.

"He's not going to be on the list ... Neko rarely knew him but I'm sure if she knew he was with me she wouldn't have a problem with seeing him."

The receptionist looked us up and down and back and forth, she was hesitant but then she took a deep breathe "Yeah go ahead she needs to hear some good news, maybe that will help her recovery process. Besides you guys are dressed too nice to do anything to harm her." I laughed nervously not knowing what Lloyd was trying to do. "Yeah.... right." I responded to the receptionist. I did know one thing I was not going to allow Lloyd to hurt her no more than he already had.

We entered the room and the first person I saw was Simone laying her head on the edge of Neko's bed right next to her head. The door startled her, she jumped up to see who was coming in the room. I wanted to say so much to her at that moment but all I could do was roll my eyes *bitch* I thought to myself. She stood up and looked me up and down she giggled and shook her head seemingly looking tired "Let me give you guys some privacy" she walked passed me and looked at me one more time before she exited. I knew what she was thinking, how could I claim to love Neko but turn around and marry a man. If I was her I would think the same thing but shit who could judge me for loving whoever it was I chose to love. My body was stiff for a minute just because I could still feel her staring at me.

I looked over at Neko, she was lying there looking so peaceful. Not feeling any pain even though she had tubes running from everywhere. We walked over closer to the bed and I could see that her face was swollen really bad. Tears started to fill my eyes as I watched the many monitors she was hooked up to. One showing the rate of her heart and the other one controlling her breathing. I looked down and watched her chest moving in and out every time the monitor clicked a certain way. I stood back as Lloyd walked up to her bedside. My heart began to pound as I listened to him talk to her not giving a fuck what he said to her. It was like he was visibly jealous of Neko.

"Yeah what up big baller dis ya boy ... you got lucky nigga cause you wasn't suppose to make it dis far. What goes around comes around huh yeah I believe in dat Karma shit nigga and you deserve erthang you got cause you's a hoe ass nigga. It's funny how da niggas whe tried to kill me spoke yo name in the process and den no sooner den you think I'm gone you start fuckin my girl.... well guess what nigga I fucked yo girl not once but several times ... got yo son knowin who his real daddy is and I wifed yo bitch nigga how you like dat shit. Now erthang dat used to be yours got my mark on it. Fuck Neko's world it's all about Lloyd. Remember we used to always say whats yours is mines ... hahhaaa well nigga now we see who got the last laugh. You's a bitch and I hope you burn nigga."

The shit he had just told Neko even stung me, he stood there for a minute while Neko laid there with no signs of change. He turned towards me and said "I know you prolly wanna have some alone time wit yo girl ... I'm thru" I looked at him and shook my head Ok as he walked towards the door. Lloyd had never put his hands on me but at that moment I didn't know what was goin through his mind. His eyes just didn't look the same to me.

I walked over to Neko's bedside and I tried to take a deep breathe but I couldn't all I could do was cry harder. After listening to Lloyd I knew that he had an agenda all along and he used my dumb ass. I don't know if I was hallucinating but it seemed like as soon as she felt my presence her heart monitor changed. I held onto her hand and kissed her, the tears running down my face stopped at my lips and on her cheek. I looked up at her unable to speak any words. My heart was in so much pain just wondering what next. I picked her hand up and placed it on my heart, I shook my head in disbelief and just cried. I knew that Lloyd was outside of the door waiting for me so I didn't want to stay long. I leaned over and kissed her one more time and finally got the knot out of my throat to speak "I am soooo sorry Neko ... I am praying for you to get better soon.... I'm holding you to your word.... I love you."

Take a sneak peek at what's coming next....

If Love Could See

Introduction

I lie in the bed looking over at the mirror which so desperately awaited me to grace its presence. I took a deep breathe and stood for which seemed like an eternity before I began to walk over to the wall where the mirror hung. My steps began to get slower as a dreaded to face what would be in front of me.

There I stood, looking at what used to depict the beauty of a strong black woman. One side of my face looking as if I was the elephant mans close relative the other side seemingly untouched. I placed my hand on the battered side and refused to cry. I did this to me, how could love be so blind.I leaned in on the sink that sat under the mirror to get a closer look at myself. My mind began to wander … wander back on that night. All I could remember was opening a door. A door to a secret world my husband hid from me for years.

As I looked around the room in amasement thoughts began to fill my head. Who was this man that I was so deeply in love with and was he indeed in love with me? I walked over to a nightstand that sat next to a rocking chair to pick up a picture and I heard a noise that startled me … I jumped … glass shattered everywhere as the picture went tumbling to the floor. It was Emily … our cat; she loved to follow me around. "Oh Emily" I cried as I went to pick her up … and that's when it happened. The first blow to the head had to have been with a blount object that sent me falling to the floor. My vision became blurry and the room began to spin. I heard a voice talking to me but could not focus on the area in which it was coming from. I remember two more blows …

About the Author

I was born on the West side of Detroit in 1976 and have been writing since I was about 10 years old. My family is what holds me together and motivates me to continue to do what it is I do. I try to write about things that everyone can relate to or are at least curious about. I am excited to finally be able to reach people through my writing and to be one of the many to expand the success stories in the LGBT community. I hope that you enjoyed the book and will be looking forward to seeing much more of me.

978-0-595-45081-7
0-595-45081-4

Made in the USA
Lexington, KY
26 May 2011